TERRAPOCALYPSE

J.E. Serrano

Dedicated to

My Mother, Inez, a true natural force
My fiancé Denee, whose love turned the Reaper
My Daughter Kirstin gave me purpose
And to all the Mothers who keep us balanced, inspiration to all.

PROLOGUE

In a state, indescribable resided Twin Entities, Infinity, and Eternity. In contemplation of a creation unseen in existence, they set forth their ambitions. These Entities drew upon the trichotomy of Omniversal forces to create a sphere impelled with a force that strained the fabric of Eternity. This pressure was bored by Eternity until Infinity interceded and added to the compulsion its gravitas resulting in the birth of the Energies and laws of the Infinite and Eternal. The laws of are:

- Motion.
- Gravity.
- The strong nuclear force.
- The weak nuclear force.
- The electromagnetic force.

With these laws and energies issued forth the spirit of Life, and She is called Gia. The secrets of giving Life were instructed to her by Eternity. Gia's mandate was to go forth into their new creation and seek a place to bring forth the decree given to her. Knowing the sense of isolation, Gia would feel with her separation from the energy to matter, Eternity, in her mercy, gifted Gia so she would not suffer loneliness. The spirit of Gia explored the newly formed cosmos until she brought her gift to a planet recently cooling from an incredible bombardment of meteors. Giving thanks (Gia knew it was a gift from Eternity containing all the building materials she would need in this new reality of matter.

Embracing the third rock from a star, Gia, upon the desolate rock, expelled the gift given to her by Eternity and gave birth to a girl, and named her child Terra. She was a clumsy child and, for the first epoch, which Humanity would call The Ordovician era. They walked on quickly cooling rocks, and Gia prepared the barren body for Life. They patiently watched as ice and snow formed, then receded. Terra watched as her Mother utilized the materials offered by Eternity and soon, through celestial waters, brought in the bombardment and melting ice and, with the aid of her star, created an atmosphere. In the heart of the newly formed world, She coaxed the iron to bond, giving the planet a stable yet fluid core. That act allowed the Earth to shield herself from the harmful rays of her foster Father. The star was overjoyed to witness the Gia spirit choose his sector to set forth her mandate. Nature formed Tectonic plates, instructing and directing paths for the lava to follow. These paths began tubes that separated fast-moving flows from the slower ones, allowing for lava pooling. Soon the tubes, along with pressure being built by storing the magma collected, created mountains that served as storage facilities that Nature would utilize to create land masse. Her first attempt at initiating Life was performed in warm waters. Gia produced Marine species.

Terra marveled at her Mother's work. The only child of Gia was curious and riddled her Mother constantly with questions about her work. Though simple, Gia's first attempt was beautiful, and Terra got to play on tropical shores testing the gifts her Mother had passed down to her. The first attempt lasted about forty-five million years, but the balance was difficult to achieve because Gia had not yet mastered the equilibrium attribute. So tricky was this attribute in the realm of the material and the biological that it took the arrival Of Lucifer, who gave Gia the idea of "Instinctual behavior," Did the life forms and the weather take on behavior patterns that became easier to manage and less self-destructive. Gia suffered what later became known as five mass extinctions. The Earth knew death by Volcanos spewing sulfur into the air. Global warming was so severe that no animal could breathe. Acidification brought about the extinction of the Triassic era. Sixty-five million years ago, A meteor that was once a gift slammed into the Mother's body so hard that it extinguished the loudest, tallest, and most ferocious of all her previous attempts at life.—the Cretaceous mass extinction. As sad as it was to see her creations perish, Nature understood the lessons she derived from them. It brought forth in her final effort the birth of Humanity.

So it was written in the records of Eternity that nobly and with integrity, the spirit Gia did accomplish her mandate, setting forth her power and bringing Life. Her daughter Terra would have more difficulties with the birth of Humanity. With the rise of Humanity, Gia begged the Eternals that her now young, beautiful, and powerful daughter be allowed to govern. When asked if she had concerns about Terra being alone, Gia begged to slumber with her spirit resting in the waters that were gifted by Eternity. So it came to pass that the heart of Gia joined with the waters of the world, but not before reassuring her daughter she would never be alone, for her Mother was a part of the waters, and all Terra had to do to converse with her was to stand beside a sea shore, and her Mother would be there. Besides, she now had all of Humanity to look after, never knowing the tribulation that awaited her daughter.

CHAPTER 1

Terra's Woes

Terra struggled with a monster storm system gathering strength in the Caribbean. This beast pushed hurricane-force winds at one hundred and twenty miles an hour. What troubled Terra was the frequency of these giants. The world has always had her storms, but Mother Nature (as the mortals liked to call her) seemed more temperamental than usual. Terra noticed that since the advent of the industrial age, the abilities of mortals to increase their waste by-products had grown exponentially, and she knew the danger humanity was steering itself toward. Terra fought desperately to maintain the fragile line of balance that allowed for pathogenesis, osmosis, mitosis, and symbiosis. These are the tools Nature used to procreate and reproduce. These tools worked best under ideal conditions and suffered if conditions were imperfect.

Nature now had to contend with the war on a level never witnessed before, As Humanity split the atom and began dropping atomic weapons, irradiating the food and water supply. People were fighting for dwindling resources while the wealthy, lusting for wealth and power, took more for themselves, leaving the rest of the population fighting for scraps. Nature saw how the weather patterns were being affected by the Humanities pollution of the skies, pouring thirty-two point one billion metric tons of industrial and fossil fuels into once blue skies. Humanity has had difficulty admitting they are part of Nature for reasons unknown to Terra. Instead, they invented stories of magically springing from dust or air; one theory suggested intelligent beings planted them here. Admittedly, although the last notion may have been closer to the truth, it would have been misunderstood if made known. Modern Man, who seemed more enthralled by destruction than awed by creativity, had developed weapons that knocked on the door of annihilation. In splitting the atom, humans evolved Nuclear capabilities that could devastate the entire planet and all Life in a single day.

Humanity had become powerful enough to destroy all Life with nothing more than a gesture. Massive oil spills that were partly responsible for drilling into the bowels of the Earth, sucking out crude oil, or their mode of transport suffer accidents that lead to ships spilling their cargo, Polluting our waterways and shores. The dumping of medical waste slowly infiltrates our water tables, exposing citizens to various illnesses, and finally, in a fit of insanity, humans have unlocked biological warfare. The balance was quickly eroding as Humanity continued pouring, dumping, spilling, and burning their pollutants into the planet's air, oceans, and bowels. Burying garbage, medical waste, and radioactive materials in caves, poorly managed dump sites, and discontinued mine shafts. As technology increased, awareness of its impact also increased. This tiny sliver of hope was depleted of tangible results as humans prioritize immediate comfort and convenience above logical long-term forecasting that might interfere with profit. This mindset allowed big corporations to lobby politically to block and lay sanctions against companies that supported any environmentalist movement. The Earth had survived mass extinctions before, but this could be the first instigated by its inhabitants. Terra knew that unless the humans began to think differently, all would be lost, and the great work of her Mother, the gift of the eternal and infinite, would have been wasted on a selfish species that she was sorry she had ever nurtured. Shaking her head angrily, Nature knew she could never give up on her children; they were all she had. Humans, however, had no such feelings. In their shortsightedness, they continued to attempt to profit from the degradation of the planet. As the polar ice caps melted, countries began to bicker over territorial, mineral, and waterway rights. Terra observed the fighting of nations with diminishing compassion. How does one feel pity for another when that other is doing everything possible to bring about calamity for all?

The air grew thicker, and the oceans sickened. Fish began to die, sea life was facing extinction, and humans responded by creating electric cars, not caring that the method used to extract the material for it to work was environmentally harmful with no credible plan for disposal of the waste produced. The situation only worsened. Oil spills were measured at fifteen thousand metric tons, averaging one point eight spills yearly. Nuclear incidents included the 1961 nuclear plant meltdown in Idaho, releasing a thousand curies of iodine-131 into the atmosphere. Adding fuel to the nuclear contamination, in 1979, the three-mile island suffered a partial meltdown. Luckily, the damage was minimal in that incident, but it was a forewarning. 1986 saw the Chernobyl disaster, where fifty and one hundred eighty-five million curies of radionuclides escaped into the atmosphere. Millions of acres of Forest and farmland were contaminated. Livestock was born deformed, and humans suffered long-term adverse effects. Terra deployed many plants as a sacrifice to help absorb some of the leakages. It was too little too late, as the Forrest was destroyed. In 2011, another nuclear plant had an incident when the Fukushima nuclear plant suffered damage from an earthquake, releasing nine hundred and forty PBq (I-131-eq) and dumping radioactive isotopes iodine-131, cesium-137, and cesium-134. The contaminants were choking the Life out of Terra. The relationship, tenuous at best with Humanity, was now straining to a breaking point where Nature felt she had to decide between her Mother's mandate (of which Terra is the successor) and her love for all the Life born and nurtured under her watch. Unknown or uncaring, Humanity was making a choice accessible to her.

In response to the deregulation of air quality, Terra shaved the magnetic shield, causing a 2003 European heat wave that killed 72,000 people. In an almost knee-jerk reaction, Humanity increased the exploitation of the planet. The once lush and, in part, still natural Amazon Forrest has been deforested an astounding thirteen and a half percent of its initial size. Terra watched as Humanity razed billions of her children. Cutting down the elders, youth, and many in their prime. The saplings, left without the canopy of the adults to protect them, are left to dry and wither an unkind and excruciating death. If humans could suffer a small portion of what they inflict upon the Natural world, the turmoil would cease.

In 2010, Nature could not reverse a warm front that caused a drought in Russia, which caused a heat wave that killed 56,000 people. None of this dissuaded Humanity's progress. Terra was disgusted at the disrespect toward her Mother. (Terra saw the waters as sacred since her Mother's spirit resided there.) Terra permitted the oceans free rein. In response

The twentieth century saw five great trans-oceanic tsunamis created by earthquakes

In 1952, one thousand five hundred people were killed in east Russia.

1960 sixteen hundred people were killed in Chile

2004, a massive tsunami took over two hundred and fifty million. India, Indonesia, Sri Lanka, Malaysia, Thailand, and Somalia. Terra stared in horror as humans ignored her anger. "If it is war they desire, I shall bring unto them a war; such has never been seen before," Terra swore as she watched the humans scrub away the evidence of their hubris.

Wrath awakened:

Awakened in fury and madness, Gia set about making proper what humanity had done. The cruise ship "Oceans Kiss" carried two thousand people in the Mediterranean, and the one thousand-foot ship sailed toward a picturesque view. Couples danced on the deck while others gambled or listened to the music played by live bands mid-ship. Sailing toward Italy, no one knew or could foresee what was coming. The passengers were invited to look upon the golden setting as the sunset. As some took up the invitation, they started to make their way to the upper deck when one of the passengers asked a crewman why the horizon was so dark. Not looking at what the passenger was referring to, the crewman stated. "That would be the evening sky, sir." He tried to hide the exasperation in his voice. "I don't think so." His companion objected. Who pointed to the horizon. The crewman looked to where her finger was pointing. "If it's just the night, as you say, shouldn't I still be able to see beyond? Maybe some lights or something. The crewman's complexion turned a gray color. The crewman bolted down the stairs toward the bridge. The passengers on the upper deck began to notice the growing darkness coming toward them. The crewman ran until he got to the bridge and shouted. "Captain! Rogue Off of the port side. The Captain ordered, "Helm, thirty degrees to port. The Helmsman reacted, echoing the orders. "Aye, sir, thirty degree's port. The ship responded as the Helmsman steered. The passengers listening to music felt the aggressive turn, the drunk passengers thought they had too much to drink, and the passengers that went to the upper deck to watch the sunset began to scream in terror as they watched a massive rogue wave bearing down on them. The swell was quickly fifty feet higher than the mast of the ship. The screams were abruptly silenced as a dark wall of water crashed upon the vessels, which capsized, sending the passengers to a watery grave.

The smokey mountains

A cloudless sky kissed and began to burn away the low-hanging fog that was the norm for these parts of the Carolinas.

A tall, rugged man, Carmel complexioned with light brown eyes, emerged from behind a thicket. He trudged through mud onto cleared lands that bordered his family's home. Terry Rogers was orphaned at the age of two. He was adopted by a loving family that saw to his needs. His adoptive parents were kind enough to tell him the truth regarding his adoption when he was old enough to understand. Unfortunately, the records of his biological family were destroyed in a flood, making it impossible for them to reveal his true ancestry. Terry realized how much love his adoptive parents must have had. Even in the late twentieth century, adopting a child from another race was uncommon. His parents were strong-willed people who taught Terry that value could only be found in people, not objects. Terry loved and respected his parents, a loving quality he intended to pass on to his family. Early in his adolescence,

Terry discovered he was increasingly drawn to Nature. His Father would often find him returning from excursions into the Forrest. Living in the foothills of the Smokey Mountains in North Carolina had a tremendous impact on the young Man.

One day, upon returning from one of his excursions, Terry sat at the table with a full bowl and hungry eyes when his Father inquired. "Boy, what might you do when you go on one of your little ventures?" Terry looked up from the bowl of cereal he was eating. "Well, pop. Between seeing all that green and hearing all the different bird calls, Oh yeah, and the sound of water running," he recalled excitedly. "The sounds of animals calling out or," Terry's frantic recollection was cut short as laughter filled the room, interrupting Terry, who, for a moment, thought he was being laughed at. "Hold a second, boy; let me catch my breath." Terry's Father begged. Always direct, as his Father taught him to be, Terry asked. "Why are you laughing at me, pop."

Winston Rogers, a stern but fair man, looked at his son with widening eyes. "Son, I was not laughing at you, no, no. I was laughing out of joy. "Huh," Terry grunted, somewhat confused. Winston sat beside his son. "The fact of the matter is that your mother and me, well, we were a bit scared that you didn't have much direction." Winston expressed. Terry looked blankly at his Father. "I'm confused," Terry admitted. "I play football for my school; I participate in church and community events; I thought you were proud of me?" Terry expressed showing concern and disappointment. "No, son." Sheryl (who had been eavesdropping on the conversation.) Terry's Mother declared as she stepped into the kitchen. "What your daddy is saying' is that it seemed as if you did all that for us, which is why when you started wandering into the woods, your daddy and I aint say nothing 'cause we thought you found something you liked to do for yourself." She clarified. Terry stood and embraced his Mother. "Mama, I'm sorry I worried you so much." Terry apologized. "Boy," Winston exclaimed. "It's us that owe you an apology. Now, you want to tell us about the journeys you love to take?" Terry whooped, jumped up, ran into the kitchen, and plopped a glass of water and a can of beer in front of his parents, who looked at each other with a smile as Terry began telling them about his explorations into Nature and some discoveries he made. His stories told Terry sat back in wonder. Watching the faraway look in their son's eyes, an intuitive awakening dawned upon Winston and Sheryl. "You thinking what I'm thinking?" Winston asked his wife. "Not sure, old man; lately, you've been questionable." Sheryl teased. "Yes, I know, but besides my bad choice in a woman, what do you?" Winston trailed off as Sheryl reached out and slapped him on the arm. "You take that back." Sheryl scowled. "Yes, mam, a thousand times," Winston begged. "Fine." Sheryl pouted. "What are you thinking, old man?" She asked. Winston looked at his son, who pretended to be daydreaming. "Terry has decided what he wants to do with his life." Winston pointed out. She nodded her head. "I think you hit the nail on the head, old man." Sheryl off-handedly complimented her husband. "You know this old man crap you keep saying' is the only thing that's old around here, and you know what? I'm only a year older than you." Terry reminded his wife, again engaging in their semi-hostile/playful banter. Sheryl fixed her husband with a laser focus while hissing. "Winston Bartholomew Rogers! You are the corniest, most unkind, ill-mannered Man I've ever had the displeasure to meet." Sheryl complained. Terry, who could not help himself, laughed. "what is wrong with you two?" He asked, exasperated. Terry tilted his head. "Wrong? boy, what you mean by wrong?" He demanded. "Well, Terry began and then fell silent. "Boy." Winston began. "Your Mama is my best friend. I don't trust anyone more than I trust her. You would be lucky to find a woman you can walk hand in hand and lay belly to belly with, but one you can go toe to toe, boy, that's a soulmate, and I pray that for you." Winston said with authority. Winston shrugged. "I meant no disrespect, pop." Terry declared. Winston nodded. "We didn't think so, son; we raised you not to be afraid to say what's on your mind." Winston conceded. "Well, your mother and I were talking, and we thought it was about time you got to moving on." Terry opened his mouth to speak but was stopped by a gesture from Winston. When you showed us what drove you, what excited you, well, your ma and I went and enrolled you at Duke for Conservationism." Winston expressed. Terry's eyes were awash with tears. Terry jumped up and embraced his Father. "Pop, thank you so much, but I can't." Terry protested. Winston slapped Terry on the back of the head. "Maybe that knocked the stupid out of your head," Winston claimed. Rubbing his head, Terry complained. "Pop Duke is expensive, and we aint got that kind of money. Winston tilted his head. "You need another smack in the back of that head, boy?" Winston asked. Terry quickly shook his head. "My money aint your money. You don't know what we do and don't have." Winston pointed out. "But you always made me get summer jobs talking about money being tight." Terry countered. "Boy, that was so you wouldn't grow up lazy. Get some sleep; this weekend, you'll be busy deciding what you want to take. We have an appointment Monday morning." Winston concluded. Terry hugged both his parents and dashed up the stairs to his room. Sheryl looked at her husband. "You sure?" She asked. Winston nodded. "The bank said they'd refinance the house," Winston informed Sheryl as she put her head against his chest as they ascended the stairs.

CHAPTER 2

The Ceremony

A silver Mercedes sliced through the rain. Vivaldi provided musical serenity as Neil Silver drove the sleek vehicle to an event honoring his work in meteorology. Neil, a weatherman on a local network, dedicated his Life to understanding the weather and its patterns. His dedication began when tragedy struck his family in a lightning storm when he was only eight. His uncle Joshua was putting the horses up before a storm hit; lightning struck him, killing him instantly. Neil was so moved by the incident, which held him mystified, terrorized, and fascinated, so much so that it became his Life's work to understand the machinations of the weather. Neil hummed as he reflected on the day he decided on his majors and how his parents reacted. "So you're going to be a weatherman?" His Father had remarked, sarcasm dripping off of the statement. "I'm going for meteorology, Dad." Neil had countered. "You know what's good about being a weatherman?" His Father asked, ignoring what his son had just said. "The only good thing about that job is that you can be wrong ninety percent of the time and not get fired." He laughed, slapping his leg. Neil sighed. "When you're right, you're right, Dad." Neil humored his Father. Grabbing his bags to leave, his Mother intercepted him at the door. Hugging him. "You know he's acting that way because he's scared for you." His Mother whispered in his ear. "I know Ma, and I loved Uncle Josh too; that's why I chose this profession to understand the why better." Neil pled. His Mother hugged him tighter. Listen, I knew my brother-in-law well. I'm here to tell you that his stubborn stubbornness killed him!" She stated angrily. Esther Mitchell was a determined woman with an incredibly analytical mind. She was a philosopher who had also trained in psychology. She was asked once why she wouldn't extend her field to include psychiatry. Her off-colored response was, "If I can't help them, medicate them? No thanks." She was what the men of her generation would call a "ball buster." She was a woman who did not permit anyone to take advantage of her. "Your father is afraid you'll go out half-cocked and try to surf a twister or something." Esther half-joked. Neil came upon his exit. Pulling up to the entrance, a concierge opened his car door. Stepping out of his new car, Neil allowed the feeling of accomplishment to be over him, and at that moment, he heard his Father's parting words. "Do something special, boy." Neil smiled at the memory. Entering the complex, he stopped and stared at the pageantry. "First time here?" a strong yet melodic voice asked. Neil turned to the source and saw a beautiful blonde-haired, green-eyed woman who stood five feet five inches, had an athletic build, and was pale-complexioned. The beautiful woman held out her hand. "Sally Mitchell." Neil took her warm hand in his, gently shaking it. "Neil, Neil Silvers." He said, introducing himself. Diane smiled and responded. "I know." she released his hand and walked away smiling. Niel stood with a dumbfounded expression on his face. A moment later, he was approached. "Doctor Silvers?" A well-dressed man asked. Terry nodded. "Yes." The well-dressed gentleman extended his hand. "I'm Mark Wells. I work for N.O.A.A., and I was wondering if you would be so kind as to give me a few moments of your time after the ceremony?" The Doctor inquired. Niel nodded. "Of course." He agreed. The event went as planned; the president of Duke University stood at the podium, praising Neil's work. "When I met Neil, he was ambitious and excited to crack what he called "The Mother's Code." Admittedly, many in the field thought it to be a philosophizing of the science, but Neil was adamant that if we put his theory to the test, it would be validated. Strangely enough, when tested, the results were precisely what Neil said it would be. How did we explain it? Well, we can't. Scientifically speaking, his theory should not yield any results, yet they did. Doctor Silvers, The President, swiveled his head, looking directly at Neil. My wife and I are going on vacation next week, and we're wondering if you would be so kind as to order us a week of clear skies and warm weather?" The President of Duke joked. "And now I'd like to bring to the stage the man who introduced a new outlook to not only meteorology but possibly all forms of conservation, Doctor Neil Silver." The audience stood and applauded. Neil made his way to the stage. He smiled and waved to people he didn't know. One woman noticed his discomfort as she had noticed his youth. At the Neil stood a moment. "I want to begin by thanking my Mother and Father, who supported me. I would also extend my gratitude to Doctor Silas for allowing me to test an unproven theory I had thought of; thank you, sir." Terry nodded to his colleague, who nodded in recognition. "My theory, to put it in a nutshell, is simple. The Earth is a living organism. We know that the Earth gives and sustains Life, but that is not what I mean. What I mean is the Earth is a living, breathing, thinking entity, and if we don't listen to what she is saying with her increased severe weather activity, we may be the only species that drove itself into extinction. The crowd fell quiet.

Someone in the audience stood. "Doctor Mansfield, World Wildlife Federation." The famous conservationist introduced himself. I would like to know what verification method you employed to quantify your results?" Neil heard the dismissive tone in the question. Neil smiled. "The same as any science technique, field test, observe, replicate," Terry responded promptly. "Yes, but that only describes the methodology." The Doctor countered. "Isn't that what you asked?" Terry asked. Doctor Mansfield nodded. "Yes, I suppose it is." He replied, sitting down. Another man stood. "My name is Mark Renault, and I'm just curious about the predictive portion of your report; you claim that within the next ten years, because of climate change due to the overuse of petroleum products, our shoreline cities will suffer flooding events?" Renault's voice raised in rebellion. "No, sir," Neil replied. "I said they would be submerged."

En garde

The audience grumbled in dismay as the questioner continued. "I'm I to understand that you're telling us that our coastal cities will be submerged? SUBMERGED? Seriously, Doctor, how can anyone take you seriously when you keep saying that," Doctor Silver raised his hand to quiet the murmuring that began. "Excuse me, Mister Renault, but you keep saying, I say. I'm telling you that I'm not saying anything. It's the Earth herself telling us." Neil insisted. "Oh, now you have a direct line to the earth?" Renault asked incredulously. Neil tilted his head. "Who is it that you represent?" He inquired. "I represent the B.D.R. consortium." He exclaimed. Neil shook his head.

"Ladies and gentlemen, I would point you to a large part of the problem right there." Doctor Silver accused. He was pointing to Renault. "That is a gross and slanderous characterization of an organization that brought you fuel for your cars, home heat, plastics, and medicines. You may certainly crawl into a cave if you wish, but I think the rest of civilization will not join you as they love their air-conditioning and heating more than the negligible effects of a temporary flux in the weather." Renault protested. Neil peered at Renault intensely. "There is no doubt that petroleum provided all that, but the question becomes, at what cost?" Neil probed. Renault snickered. "The cost? Cool air in the summer and warm air in the winter. He replied evasively. Neil shook his head. "How disingenuous of you. That has to be one of the most evasive responses I've had the displeasure of hearing, Mister Renault. If your medicine is so good for us, why was the A.M.A. bribed to state that natural medicines were ineffective? Who toxified our air, water, and Earth? That would be your industry." Neil rebuked. Renault smiled. "Perhaps, but we cannot be held responsible for past mistakes nevertheless." He countered.

"Mister Renault." Neil began. "Can we admit that the petroleum industries would never admit to the effects of climate change?" Staying in character, Renault smoothly replied. "We admit that if it were not for our research, we would still travel by horse-drawn carriages, read by candlelight," Neil interjected Renault's rant. "Mister Renault, please. We are all too familiar with the denial speeches, but I assure you, sir, Nature shall rebuke all of your works; she is furious and in fury shall rise." Silver declared. The oil representative looked offended. "You speak to me, sir, as if I'm a common criminal, and I take offense to that." Renault declared. Silver crossed his arms, staring at the Rep. "I apologize for offending your delicate sensitivities." Silver mocked in return. Renault sat down and made a phone call.

"Are there any more questions?" Neil asked. "So what is the solution?" A familiar voice inquired. Neil squinted into the audience. "Would you please identify yourself?" Neil requested. "Yes sir, my name is Sally Mitchell, and I've been listening to what you've been saying, and I'm fascinated that you think of the earth as a living sentient being." Neil recognized the soft-spoken voice. "The answer to your question is yes, Mrs. Mitchell, I think the Earth is sentient," Neil said with a smile that she found appealing. "I'm sorry, Doctor Rogers, but aren't you concerned at being ridiculed by the rest of the scientific community? Oh, and it's Miss Mitchell." Sally responded coyly. Neil's smile deepened. "No, Miss Mitchell, not at all. As a scientist, I must explore, without bias, any possibility that leads to a credible solution to the question posed. Not. I repeat, Not answers that are for the sake of convenience, profits, or politics. Science may be the last bastion of uncorrupted information, and I intend to continue to act accordingly."

Neil insisted. Unknown to Neil, the passion in his voice stirred the pit of Sally's gut, and she watched how this electrically charged Man was convinced he was right. Sally heard mumblings of dissent and accusations of absurdities. She was shocked at the resistance thrown at the young scientist, yet she watched. Sally watched as he deftly avoided the charge of working for a conservationist Pac. She listened as Neil was accused of accepting pay-offs from a clean air Pac representative from the oil industry. All the time, Neil smiled. "Ladies and gentlemen, I want to thank you for the recognition, your precious time and patience, and Mister Renault, thank you for the attack upon my integrity and to those that refuse to look at the facts the very world is presenting to you, I will be accepting apologies throughout the upcoming ordeals, thank you." Neil gave a short bow to a smattering of applause, the loudest coming from Sally.

"Doctor Mitchell?" Sally turned. Doctor Weinstein?" She gasped in surprise, embracing him. "How are you? it's been a while." Sally exclaimed. "Yes, it has been a while. I see you're still trying to save the world." He said playfully. She smiled shyly. "Yes, in fact, I am," Sally exclaimed proudly. "Excellent goal." Weinstein agreed. "But my dear, I would warn you about who you ally yourself with." He subtly warned. Sally smiled to hide her resentment at what sounded like a threat to her. "I'm only saying that a particular doctor has written some papers that border the ridiculous. Is the Earth alive? For god's sake, it's utter nonsense." Weinstein complained disdainfully. An inner voice told her not to be combative, and Sally paid heed to that voice and smiled sweetly. "You know me, professor, I love looking at new ideas." Sally deflected. Weinstein smiled. "Of course, you always were unafraid to look at something new." He acknowledged. "I'm glad that is all it is for you. Frankly dear, I don't see much of a future for our dear Doctor Rogers." Weinstein exclaimed. Sally gave him another hug. It was good to see you again, my old mentor." Weinstein protested. "Hey, I'm not that old. Sally giggled. "I'm only teasing; you'll always be the man, professor," Sally claimed. Weinstein sighed. "If only that were true, my dear. Sally smiled as she turned to try to catch Doctor Rogers before he left.

Dissension

The audience grumbled in dismay as the questioner continued. "I'm I to understand that you're telling us that our coastal cities will be submerged? SUBMERGED? Seriously, Doctor, how can anyone take you seriously when you keep saying that," Doctor Silver raised his hand to quiet the murmuring that began. "Excuse me, Mister Renault, but you keep saying, I say. I'm telling you that I'm not saying anything. It's the Earth herself telling us." Neil insisted. "Oh, now you have a direct line to the earth?" Renault asked incredulously. Neil tilted his head. "Who is it that you represent?" He inquired. "I represent the B.D.R. consortium." He exclaimed. Neil shook his head.

"Ladies and gentlemen, I would point you to a large part of the problem right there." Doctor Silver accused. He was pointing to Renault. "That is a gross and slanderous characterization of an organization that brought you fuel for your cars, home heat, plastics, and medicines.

You may undoubtedly crawl into a cave if you wish, but I think the rest of civilization will not join you as they love their air-conditioning and heating more than the negligible effects of a temporary flux in the weather." Renault protested. Neil peered at Renault intensely. "There is no doubt that petroleum provided all that, but the question becomes, at what cost?" Neil probed. Renault snickered. "The cost? Cool air in the summer and warm air in the winter. He replied evasively. Neil shook his head. "How disingenuous of you. That has to be one of the most evasive responses I've had the displeasure of hearing, Mister Renault. The facts remain your air medicine; if it's so good for us, who was the A.M.A. bribed to state that natural medicines were ineffective? Or poisoned our air, water, and Earth? That would be your industry." Neil rebuked. Renault smiled. "Perhaps, but true nevertheless."

"Mister Renault." Neil began. "Can we admit that the petroleum industries would never admit to the effects of climate change?" Staying in character, Renault smoothly replied. "We admit that if it were not for our research, we would still travel by horse-drawn carriages, read by candlelight," Neil interjected Renault's rant. "Mister Renault, please. We are all too familiar with the denial speeches, but I assure you, sir, Nature shall rebuke all of your works; she is furious and in fury shall rise." Silver declared. The oil representative looked offended. "You speak to me, sir, as if I'm a common criminal, and I take offense to that." Renault declared. Silver crossed his arms, staring at the Rep. "I apologize for offending your delicate sensitivities." Silver mocked in return. Renault sat down and made a phone call.

"Are there any more questions?" Neil asked. "So what is the solution?" A familiar voice inquired. Neil squinted into the audience. "Would you please identify yourself?" Neil requested. "Yes sir, my name is Sally Mitchell, and I've been listening to what you've been saying, and I'm fascinated that you think of the earth as a living sentient being." Neil recognized the soft-spoken voice. "The answer to your question is yes, Mrs. Mitchell, I think the Earth is sentient," Neil said with a smile that she found appealing. "I'm sorry, Doctor Silver, but aren't you concerned about being ridiculed by the rest of the scientific community? Oh, and it's Miss Mitchell." Sally responded coyly. Neil's smile deepened. "No, Miss Mitchell, not at all. As a scientist, I must explore, without bias, any possibility that leads to a credible solution to the question posed. Not. I repeat, Not answers that are for the sake of convenience, profits, or politics. Science may be the last bastion of uncorrupted information, and I intend to continue to act accordingly."

Neil insisted. Unknown to Neil, the passion in his voice stirred the pit of Sally's gut, and she watched how this electrically charged Man was convinced he was right. Sally heard mumblings of dissent and accusations of absurdities. She was shocked at the resistance thrown at the young scientist, yet she watched. Sally watched as he deftly avoided the charge of working for a conservationist Pac. She listened as Neil was accused of accepting pay-offs from a clean air Pac representative from the oil industry. All the time, Neil smiled. "Ladies and gentlemen, I want to thank you for the recognition, your precious time and patience, and Mister Renault, thank you for the attack upon my integrity and to those that refuse to look at the facts the very world is presenting to you, I will be accepting apologies throughout the upcoming ordeals, thank you." Neil gave a short bow to a smattering of applause, the loudest coming from Sally.

"Doctor Mitchell?" A voice called her name. Sally turned to see an old colleague. Doctor Weinstein?" She gasped in surprise, embracing him. "How are you? it's been a while." Sally exclaimed. "Yes, it has been a while. I see you're still trying to save the world." He said playfully. She smiled shyly. "Yes, in fact, I am," Sally exclaimed proudly. "Excellent goal." Weinstein agreed. "But my dear, I would warn you about who you ally yourself with." He subtly warned. Sally smiled to hide her resentment at what sounded like a threat to her. "I'm only saying that a particular doctor has written some papers that border the ridiculous. Is the Earth alive? For god's sake, it's utter nonsense." Weinstein complained disdainfully. An inner voice told her not to be combative, and Sally paid heed to that voice and smiled sweetly. "You know me, professor, I love looking at new ideas." Sally deflected. Weinstein smiled. "Of course, you always were unafraid to look at something new." He acknowledged. "I'm glad that is all it is for you. Frankly, dear, I don't see much of a future for Doctor Silver." Weinstein exclaimed. Sally gave him another hug. It was good to see you again, my old mentor." Weinstein protested. "Hey, I'm not that old. Sally giggled. "I'm only teasing; you'll always be the Man, professor," Sally claimed. Weinstein sighed. "If only that were true, my dear. Sally smiled as she turned to try to catch Doctor Silver before he left. Seeing him head to an exit, she moved to intercept him. Looking at him, Sally fancied herself working beside him. She shook away the silly daydream. Sally waved to another colleague as she closed the gap between herself and Doctor Silver. She hoped he would be as forthright in person and all he was bantering about was not just for fundraising. Sally stopped short. *What if all of this reflecting I've been doing is nothing more than a fantasy? They say you should never meet your heroes.*

Sally pondered. Looking up, she realized The Doctor would leave before she could get to him. "Goddamn distractions!" Sally muttered aloud. "Excuse me?" She called out loudly. Niel was about to open the door when he heard Sally's outburst and stopped to look at her. Sally walked over to him. "Excuse my brashness, Doctor, but I was captivated by some of your theories." Niel smiled. Sally returned the smile. After a moment of uncomfortable silence, Niel inquired. "Would you like to join me in a cup of tea?" He invited. Sally's smile deepened. "That would be nice," Sally responded shyly.

CHAPTER 3
Pride

Winston had a huge smile on his face. He folded the letter he had just read and looked at his beloved Smokey Mountains. Sheryl joined him on the porch, handing him a cup of coffee. A bright Cardinal sang its beautiful song in search of a mate. The sky's blue was sharp; the air was warm with a gentle breeze blowing. "You used to sing to me like that back in the day," Sheryl claimed as the cardinal sang. Winston found it sweet that she would say such a thing, but it was sentimental foolishness. "Woman, if you said I sang like a blue jay, that would be truthful," Winston stated. "Hmph!" Sheryl protested. "You remember things the way you want; you're grouchy because we missed Terry's event." She pointed out. Winston shrugged. "That might be, but according to this," Winston pulled out the letter he just read and gave it to Sheryl. Seeing Terry's handwriting, she snatched it. "You've been holding out on me?" She accused. "Listen here, you crazy woman, the mailman dropped it off this morning. Don't blame me because you wanted to sleep late." Winston complained, but Sheryl was into her son's letter. Her face reflects on how each letter passage brought a different response." Winston, our boy, stood before the scientific community and told them they didn't know what they were discussing?" She asked, shocked and deeply concerned. "Yep, sounds about right," Winston confirmed. "What is that foolish boy doing? He'll never find work if he bad mouths other folks' work; he won't be able to find a job." She worried. "Okay, slow down, missy," Winston directed. "If you keep reading, you'll see he has an assignment in Florida." Winston pointed out. "Florida?! What in the hell is he going to do in Florida?" Sheryl demanded. "I'd imagine whatever his education prepared him for. Remember, darling, money has never been important to our boy. If he's going to make his mark in his world, he has to find something everyone else thinks of in a wrong way and prove them wrong." Winston explained. Sheryl glared at him. "I know that old fool. I'm just concerned because if he separates, who will help him? Either your colleagues believe in your work, or the public does. That is how our work gets funded, and no matter how much Terry hates the corporate world, they are major contributors." She proclaimed. "Yeah, you're right," Winston agreed. "Regarding the contribution part, corporations contribute when the research supports their actions or products." Winston objected. "Yes, dear," Sheryl capitulated, but he will still need funding to do his work and hopefully meet someone." She responded in a Motherly fashion. Winston burst into laughter. Sheryl shot him a look. "What are you laughing at?" She challenged. With a smirk, Winston responded. "Keep reading." He replied. Doing as directed, Sheryl's face lit up. "He met a girl?!" She squeaked. "A woman." Winston corrected. "A scientist just like him." Winston pointed out. "And Jewish." Sheryl piped. "And?" Winston demanded. "I've never known you to be racist, Sheryl," Winston stated in a shocked tone. "I'm not you idiot; I married you." She stated sarcastically. "What the hell," He began. "Yeah," Sheryl continued. "Yeah, you were so damned ugly my folks thought I was marrying outside my species." She snapped at him. Sher, you're so full of shit." Winston rebuked. "Ohh, you don't remember how you used to dress or how you used to hang out with your friends all hours of the night, causing all kinds of ruckus?" Sheryl reminded him. "Yeah, well, Terry got a girl." Winston cheered weakly. "A woman." Sheryl corrected. "A woman," Winston said happily. "What do you think about visiting him when he's in Florida?" Sheryl asked innocently. Winston returned the question with a withering look Sheryl didn't appreciate. "What's with the look?"

She asked. "What look?" Winston asked evasively. "What look? The evil eye you gave me, and don't deny it, Winston Bartholomew Rodgers!" Sheryl warned. "Winston swore the blood of the Cherokee ran through this woman. "Fine, woman, you want to get into this?" Winston asked seriously. In response, Sheryl rolled her sleeves up. "Fine. You might not have noticed, but I've been trying to get you to come camping with me for years, except this past couple of days because I figured out you didn't want to go," Winston began. "Took you long enough," Sheryl mumbled. Winston squinted at his wife. "So it wasn't the cold, uncomfortable ground or ticks?" Winston probed. "Oh dear god, yes, it was all those things." She confirmed. Winston nodded. "I see, but now that it's your boy, you're willing to endure all that discomfort and bug bites?" Terry asked with an edge to his voice. Sheryl tilted her head back, hearing the tone in his voice. "Okay, first, lose the edge; secondly, hell no. What made you think that?" She asked, surprised. "Sheryl, you know that boy is in Florida?" Winston queried. With a straight face, she confirmed that she did. "And you know he's in the field?" Winston continued. "I do," Sheryl responded, unswayed by her husband's logic. "And you know he's in the Everglades, bugs, giant mosquitos, man-eating ticks, and gators." Winston ended dramatically. "Uh-huh. Do you know what else Florida has? Hotels," She said triumphantly. Winston cocked his head to the side. "Like the Everglade Hilton?" Winston asked, sounding perplexed. "I'd imagine so." Sheryl agreed. "We'd still have to go to his worksite; there would still be bugs." He pointed out. "Well, couldn't he come into town and have dinner with us." Winston crossed his arms. "Sheryl, you want me to tell that boy that we're coming near his job site, and we want him to set some time aside to come out of the swamps to have dinner with us?." Winston probed. Sheryl scowled at her husband. "Why'd you have to say it like that.' She complained. Winston smiled. Like what?" He inquired innocently. "Don't do that; you don't disguise the snark well." She pointed out. "When you're right, you're right." Winston feigned surrender. "I get it, Winston; I'm a smothering Mother." She snapped. Winston hugged her. "No, my dear, you're a loving Mother, and I wouldn't have you any other way. Sheryl hugged her husband. "I am so proud of our boy. "You?" Winston snapped. Tomorrow, I'm going to the barbershop and tell all the folks what kind of noise our boy is making. Sheryl squeezed Winston harder.

Silver joy

Niel Silver sat in his old overstuffed chair in a study filled with books on meteorology and weather patterns for the past twenty years he's been monitoring. Almost thirty years had passed since his speech regarding severe climate change, and the entire scientific community branded him an alarmist. Stating that his opinions had no basis. Reading a paper on climate change and seeing his former detractors nimbly dance over their mistakes. "Idiots, better late than never." He grumbled. "What's that, dear?" His wife Sally called out from the kitchen. "I'm just reading about these morons are now trying to act like they've been trying to warn us about this for years," Niel replied. Sally appeared in the doorway. "You and I know where the true research began." Sally mollified. "Ya damned right we do!" Niel exclaimed. Sally smiled at her husband. "Try not to let it upset you, dear," Niel grunted. "I just wished we weren't always playing catch-up." Niel continued complaining. Sally cocked her head to one side. "Niel, you and I know that trailblazers seldom get either credit or enjoy the fruits of their discovery; unfortunately, the people often come up behind them and categorize and implement the S.O.P. on such matters." Sally pointed out." Damn, bottom feeders." Niel spat. Sally stepped away from the door into the Study. "Don't be that way, Niel. The people who come up behind the trailblazers are just as vital as they set standards that allow for guidelines that reinforce fair and honest work and communication of new ideas. Niel let out a low whistle. "Wow, I'm thankful you never spoke that crap while we were raising Sally," Niel exclaimed, expressing relief. Sally frowned. "Too much?" Niel shook his head. "If I didn't know the contrarian you are? Then yes, way too much. Since when did you become an apologist? Sally grinned mischievously. "Since that day you gave that speech that infuriated your colleagues," Sally informed. Niel looked surprised. "Really?" He asked. "I didn't know the issues I was having with my colleagues affected you so much; I'm sorry." Niel professed. Sally laughed. "Niel, you schmuck, I knew the the information you shared was spot on. I also knew when these imbeciles finally caught up with you, they would never admit their mistake and that one day, when they report what you've been saying for years, I would need to calm you down. "Hmph. I don't feel very calm." He grunted. Sally smiled seductively as she slid into her husband's arms. "Well, perhaps I can try another well-proven method of relaxation." She whispered coyly. Niel swept his wife up. "Let's go." He said enthusiastically. He carried her off to their bedroom. The moments after lovemaking, when a couple committed to one another feels the ebb of sexual gratification and the flow of continuity because you are with your life partner, are the moments both Niel and Sally enjoyed as they felt it brought them closer to each other and Nature. "I wonder how the kid is doing?" Niel wondered aloud. Sally slapped her husband's arms. "Get out of my head; I thought the same thing." Sally exclaimed. "Okay, if you want me out of your head, you must shut off the vacancy sign." Sally elbowed Niel at the old joke. "It was about three years after they had Sally that Niel began to finish Sally's questions for her inadvertently. As an independent woman, she was not pleased with the idea she was so easily read. That is until Niel proposed their compatibility was so high that they had a natural synchronicity that allowed for non-verbal communication. As if on cue, their text notification buzzed. Picking up her phone, Sally saw it was from Sally. She excitedly showed her husband, who sat up, seeing who it was from. "Greetings, parental units." The text started. "I just want to update you on what's going on. Dad, I met this awesome Man, and he's just like you. He is on a mission to save the world. At a science convention, he recently tried to warn the scientific community that all the world's disasters could be linked to what he called 'The Gia effect.' Terry, by the way, his name is Terry. He explained that the world has a soul, and we have caused a major disruption in her harmonic frequencies, creating a dis-harmonic wave of destruction. No one wanted to hear what he had to say. It is much like the stories Mom told about your struggles, Dad. He's honest and compassionate, and I think I love him. He has been given a grant to monitor the meteorological effects of climate change in the Florida Everglades. I have also put in a grant to measure the conservation the Everglades are affecting. Don't worry, Dad, I am going for my work, not just following a man." Niel let out the breath he was holding. He looked over at Sally, who sat with tears in her eyes. "Niel, our baby is not a baby anymore." She whispered. Niel took her in his arms. "Don't be silly; no matter how old she is or whoever she calls her love, she will always be our baby." He said soothingly. "Besides, if we don't like him when we meet, we can kill him." He joked. For whatever reason, Sally broke into laughter at the statement. "I knew you'd make it right, baby." Sally nuzzled her husband's neck. "For you, kid, I'd move the world," Niel claimed in a bad Clint Eastwood impersonation. "I declare, Mister, the world is mighty big." Sally mocked in a southern drawl. "Yup." Neil agreed. "That it is, but for you, mam, It shall be done." He joked. Sally snatched the phone, texting a reply to her daughter. "Baby, Dad and I are very happy for you; just remember to take your time and be sure of your feelings. We hope to meet your young Man very soon. Dad wanted me to remind you he finds this gentleman of yours unacceptable. Our dumpsite will have a fresh body. I'm sure your Father will love him as long as he makes you happy. Do you know when you and your guy are going to visit? How long is your research going to last? Do you plan on publishing your findings? May I peruse it before you release it? The home front is the same; your Father is talking about getting a dog to walk with him. I love to, but Man doesn't take walks; he goes on adventures, and I'm not up to all that. Well, I guess that is all for now; oh, by the way, I was just nominated for a Connie. No big deal, I don't expect to win; of course, your Father says I'm a shoo-in, but he's said I was nominated the three prior times. I will keep you informed. Very happy for you, sweetheart. Love Mom & Dad." Diane hit send, overjoyed at her daughter's news.

CHAPTER 4
A Silver Lining

Neil exited the event center, happy that the ceremony was over. Neil was a bit shaken by the obtuse and close-mindedness of his colleagues. He knew his ideas were unorthodox for the scientific community but never expected the staunch opposition. Reflecting on something his foster Father had once told him, *"Boy, all the brains and no heart leaves a man cold and kind of empty inside. He'll spend the rest of his Life trying to warm and fill that emptiness. His curse is that he never will and will hurt many people on the way trying to." Neil's Father advised." Neil smiled at the memory of him.* Eli Silver was a big man. His Mother, Rebecca, would call him her giant Maccabee. Raised in the traditions of his people, he was a humble yet powerfully built man. Unlike his wife, he limited his education to more traditional values. The Man could repair almost anything. He was both an artisan and mechanic, poet and philosopher. Neil was jolted from his memories by a familiar voice. "Brilliant!" She exclaimed. For the first time that evening, Neil smiled a genuine smile. "Well, hello." He replied, glad to see her. "Doctor, I must tell you how impressed I was by your theory." She said, emoting enthusiasm. Neil looked confused. "Excuse me, Sally, right?" Neil sought confirmation.

Sally nodded. Sally Mitchell." She concurred. "Sally, I'm just slightly confused as I only had an opportunity to touch on the issue briefly." Neil clarified. Sally nodded. "Yes, that is true." She agreed. Neil tilted his head at Sally as if asking for more information. Seeming to enjoy the moment, Sally avoided the question. "I wonder about your concern for your safety, Doctor?" Neil began sauntering, enjoying the weather but the company even more. "Why would you have such concerns, Doctor?" Neil inquired. "Do you realize you insulted a Lobbyist of a powerful energy consortium?" Sally asked. Neil shrugged. "And?" He asked off-handedly. Sally's mouth fell open. "Doctor," She began before Neil interjected. "Please, call me Neil." Sally pouted. "I can't believe you're naive, Neil, and I know you're not stupid." Sally began, building steam at the seeming carelessness of the Man. "I seemed to have upset you," Neil observed. Sally shot him a glance. "Ya think?" She asked sarcastically, abruptly turning away from him. Neil's face softened. "It was not my intention to upset you. After a moment of uncomfortable silence, Neil queried. "May I ask why are you so upset?" He asked softly. "Would you first tell me why you spoke like you did today, with such audacity and recklessness?" She probed. Neil considered his words. "I was raised by a wise man who taught me to be "Chazak." Not to allow the shadow of fear to overwhelm my responsibility on what needs to be done in Life."

Sally realized she was in awe of this Man's courage and, frankly, was very easy on the eyes. "Chazak?" She asked, seeking clarification. Neil grinned at her curiosity. "It means to be strong, courageous." Sally returned his grin. "I, too, have a Hebrew ancestry, but my Mother and Father are not practitioners of the faith," Sally admitted. Neil laughed, thinking what his Mother would say to that remark. "What's so funny? She asked. "Oh, I was just thinking how my Mother would have responded to what you said," Neil answered. "Oh, and what would that have been? Sally asked curiously. "Practice? How does one practice their blood?" Neil shared. "Wow," Sally reacted. "Your Mom was deep."

Neil nodded in agreement. "Frighteningly so." Neil agreed. They continued walking and sharing information on one another's goals and desires. Hearing some of Neil's aspirations left Sally mesmerized by the grandiosity of it all. "So you want to change the world?" Sally inquired. Neil chuckled. "No, not at all. The very notion seems far-reaching. No,

I want to change our understanding of the world." Neil retorted. Sally tilted her head in disagreement. "One could argue that an understanding would indeed change the world as we would cut back on actions that are destructive to our world." Sally pointed out. Neil smiled. "I suppose you're right." He agreed. "Neil," Sally began. "I know your work far exceeds any prior work in your field, but," Neil interjected. "Excuse me for interrupting, but this is the second time you've referred to my work, and when I asked you about your knowledge about it, you just glossed over any response." Sally looked away shyly. "The fact of the matter, Neil, is that It wasn't by accident I am here tonight. I read your report on "Global fluctuations and their impact on modern society.""

Sally shared. She looked back at Neil, who was looking at her anxiously. Afraid that this intelligent, beautiful woman thought he was crazy. "Genius," Sally whispered as if reading his mind. "Thank you, Sally," Neil whispered in return. "Seriously, Neil, I've never read such depth and clarity. It is one of the reasons I'm so concerned for you." Sally expressed her worry. "I'm afraid someone powerful is going to read it and realize you stumbled unto something they may have already known or believed and don't want anyone else to know for fear of losing their fortunes."

Sally posed seriously." Neil grinned. "I never even thought of the possibility of that." He admitted. Sally looked at him with concern. "If you accept that you just may have made a target of yourself, why are you smiling?" She asked, worried about his seeming lack of care for his safety. "I'm smiling because I don't think I have to face it alone. That is, if I'm reading this weather pattern correctly?" Neil, in part, joked. Sally looked into his eyes. "Never again if you wish?" She confirmed. Neil's grin grew to an ear-to-ear smile. "Yes, mam, I do wish," Neil responded, overjoyed at the outcome of this evening.

Fate entwined

The following spring was a busy one as Niel finalized his affairs. He had submitted a proposal for a study of the meteorological effects of climate change upon the Florida ever-glades. Although it was busy putting his affairs in order. The day after Sally agreed to a committed relationship, the task became what some would call a "blissful pain." the red tape was gathered and then unwound as all of the paperwork so Sally could continue her work. The pain derived from the administrative end of things as Niel deplored paperwork. The bliss came from the fact that Niel, despite his dedication and belief, was despondent over the fact that most of his scientific findings were open to interpretation. The only reason that was so was that the Nature of the subject being studied was Nature, and Nature is fluid, not fixed, making exact calculations extremely difficult. Lucky for Niel, the force of chance placed a beautiful, knowledgeable person with just enough independence not to buy into the status quo. After their initial meeting, they saw each other daily, and as they became better acquainted, Niel began to see the brilliance that was her intelligence. When Niel was pouring over charts of the Everglades, Sally suggested compiling her records of Conservationism with his meteorological forecasts to show a correlation of patterns that reveal intent when taken from an objective perspective. Niel smiled at the memory. "Good luck indeed." He mused. "Hey, air for brains, whatcha doin?" Niel fought the grin that threatened his look of repose. "Hey, bug breath." He responded cooly. Another aspect of his relationship with Sally that he loved. Although well respected in their fields, Sally's parents raised her with a down-to-earth thing about her that Niel loved. Her playful insults brought spice to their relationship, and for that, Niel was grateful. "Do me a favor, babe?" Sally asked. Niel looked at her. "Of course, babe, whatcha need?" He asked, smiling playfully. "The next time," Sally began. "Remember, I'm a conservationist, not an entomologist." She pointed out. Niel shrugged. "Yeah, I knew that." He pointed out. Sally tilted her head in confusion. "Yeah, it's just that you called me bug breath." She reminded him, or so she thought. Niel smiled. "And?" Niel continued obtusely. Sally folded her arms. "Okay, what is this?" She demanded. Niels brows furrowed. "What is what?" Niel demanded. Sally returned the eye furrow. "This! All this!" She demanded in a pitched voice. Unable to contain himself, Niel burst into laughter. Sally began stomping. "What the hell is so funny, and what the hell are you laughing at?" She demanded. Niel tried to stop laughing but failed. "Okay, you got ten seconds to stop laughing, or it gonna get," Niel embraced her. "Okay, first, you started it, second, you caught me off guard with the airhead comment, and I couldn't think of a comeback, so I looked to irritate you instead." Niel explained. Sally pursed her lips. "You ass." She asserted. "Yes, dear, I'm a sore loser." Sally learned her Man was a born fighter and, like she, was a devotee to the cause of repairing the rift between Nature, as her sentient self, and humanity. The couple worked frantically to ensure everything was in order. Niel knew he had to make plans in case Sally's observations that they could be making potent enemies came to fruition. Niel was willing to face all opposition when he was by himself, but with Sally, he couldn't leave it to chance. He was hypocritical since he acknowledged Chance as the vehicle where he met Sally. He knew the Nature of chance, and it was one of unreliability. Niel also knew that Sally must never learn of the precautions he was taking for her as she would interpret it as Niel having to protect her, and few things make her as angry as someone thinking of her as weak and in need of protection. She was kind enough to point it out to Niel as one day, during one of their dates, a young man told her that she should lose the dweeb (referring to Niel) and get with him. Before Niel could say anything, Sally stood and walked over to where the Man sat. She picked up the Man's beer and poured it over his head while saying. "You are barbaric, unseemly, and rude, while that Man sitting over there, who you referred to as a dweeb, is a gentleman. Where kindness and civility are active participants in his Life, yours is full of jealousy and envy for those who have what you wish for. If you truly want a meaningful relationship, start acting meaningfully and stop acting like a childish jerk." She concluded. During her speech, the Man stood in disbelief, but instead of anger, the Man looked ashamed. Seeing this, Sally probed. "It all begins with an act of contrition. Sally looked at Niel. The Man took the meaning, walked over to Niel, and extended his hand. "Sir, I'd like to apologize for my rude behavior. The words of your beautiful woman pierced my heart because it was filled with truth. I hope you can accept my apology." Niel took the extended hand and shook it. "Thank you, sir. It takes an incredible amount of courage to say what you said." Niel acknowledged. Or the stinging truth." The Man added. "Or that." Niel concurred. "Sometimes separating ourselves from a comfortable truth can be extremely difficult." Niel pointed out. The young Man nodded. "While that is undoubtedly true, it is no excuse;

as scientists, we should never scoff at what seems new." The young Man pointed out. Niel looked the young Man up and down before asking. "What is your name." He inquired. The young Man smiled. "Roger Fleming." The Man shared. "May I ask your field?" Niel probed. "Well," Roger began. "I started in oceanography, changed to ichthyology, and settled on marine biology," Roger concluded. "At least you stayed in a relevant field." Niel expressed. "Relevant to what?" Roger inquired. "To one another. Most young students pick studies where the first has nothing to do with their secondaries. At least you are consistent with your studies of the Oceans," Niel pointed out. Rogers's grin grew wider. "I never thought of it that way. My Father kept saying I was wasting time jumping from one major to another." He complained. Niel shrugged. "Dads want what's best for their children." Niel acknowledged. Roger grunted. "Or what they think is best. Niel nodded, chuckling. "Yes, on that, you are correct." The silence passed as Niel knew this young Man had something to say. His patience was rewarded a moment later when Roger asked. "Professor, do you think the world is under siege?" Niel studied Roger a moment. "Where are you now regarding getting your degree?" He inquired. "I get my bachelor's degree next year," Niel interjected. Niel looked back at Sally, who stood patiently while the two spoke. "This," Niel said by way of introduction. "Is Sally. We plan a trip to the Everglades to study the effects of climate change. If you wish, I could use an assistant with working knowledge of the oceans and their machinations. "Really? I mean, seriously?." Roger was glowing. "Yes, sir! I would love the opportunity." He nearly gasped. "Very well. keep your grades up, and you can join us in the Everglades when your semester ends." Roger cocked his head slightly. "Pay?" He inquired hopefully. Niel cocked his head, mirroring Roger. "Internship," Niel said with the same tone Roger used. "Screw it, I'm in." Niel shook his hand. "Keep the grades up, and we'll see you in six months or so," Niel said. One could see the excitement in Rogers's steps as he walked away. "Another one in the team?" Sally asked. Niel, who was still looking at Roger as he began to do small dance steps. Turning to Sally, he responded. "Indeed it does."

CHAPTER 5
The Everglades

It was another hot day in Florida, and Neil was ecstatic. The jubilation was because his experiment on coastal deterioration due to inclement weather produced results confirming his theory of advanced climate change. "Did it confirm your expectations, honey?" Sally asked. Neil looked back at his bride, smiling. She jumped into his arms. "See," She quipped. "I told you it was going to confirm your theory. "Yes, my love, but there is a difference between proving a theory and having it accepted." Neil complained. "That is true." She acknowledged. "How did your day go?" Neil asked his wife. "My experiments are equally disturbing." She related. "In what way? Neil asked. "Well, I've taken various samples of surface and underground water as well as some root samples, and I've found an increase in acidity. The glycosides and proteins have been undergoing a subtle shift on a molecular scale, increasing their toxicity to humans." Sally posed. Neil's expression revealed confusion. "Harmful to humans?" He repeated. Sally nodded. "Only humans." She clarified. "Hmm, that's odd." Neil replied, feeling the gravity of an unknown situation. "What are you thinking?" She inquired. Neil took a moment, reflecting on his history lessons. Neil stared off into the distance while reflecting. Sally gave her husband time to think. Being a fellow academic, she was familiar with this intense moment of concentration. "I got it." Neil uttered, snapping back to the present. "What is it, dear?" An excited Sally inquired. "Well." Neil began. "I was trying to remember where I had seen such patterns before," Neil explained haltingly, which slightly irritated his anxious wife. "Neil!" She demanded he get on with it. "Well, it struck me that I didn't recognize it because I had never seen it except in a book." Neil exclaimed. A frustrated Sally narrowed her eyes, squinting at Neil. The meteorologist looked at his wife. "Extinction events." Neil said. Sally staggered back as if punched in the stomach. "Oh, my god." She silently mouthed. Neil nodded. She saw it clear as day now. This brilliant Man saw what no one else saw, which terrified her. "I see it. It looks like a mix of Permian and Triassic events jammed together." She realized. Neil looked perplexed. "What's on your mind, honey?" Sally inquired. Her husband looked at her with tears in his eyes. Sally was taken aback seeing him so upset. "Tell me, how can I help?" She pled. Neil looked away. "I can't think of anyone we can trust with this information." He said sadly. Sally knew what her husband meant. Governments would set up programs for the Select few. Hand-picked individuals whom the government felt were necessary for the continuity of power. The rich would do the same, using their vast wealth as a bargaining chip to ensure they survive, leaving the masses to die. Tears formed in Sally's eyes as well. Neil embraced his wife. "Don't worry, my love; we'll figure something out." Neil exclaimed with little confidence. "But how can you be so sure?" Sally asked. Neil smiled broadly. "Because I have the brightest girl by my side." Neil cooed. Sally pushed away from his hug. "Stop. I'm serious, Neil, we have to tell someone or…" She left the sentence uncompleted. Neil nodded. "Yes, dear, I know." He agreed. The sun was beginning to set as the couple made their way to the elevated platform that served as their campground. Neil designed the simple platform, insisting they would not sleep at ground level in a swamp. They made tender love that night with the knowledge that a terrible shadow could be hanging over humanity's heads, and these two scientists were the only people in a world of billions aware of what might happen. Sally and Neil continued their experiments in the Everglades for the next couple of months before coming home one evening from collecting his never-ending sample gathering (or, as Neil called it, "Data collections. he noticed his wife was getting a little chubby. Having enough sense not to say anything crass, Neil said nothing. As time passed, He noticed his wife was not her usual energetic self. When asked if she felt okay, she gave her husband a look that would have frozen hot water. Seeing her piercing eyes look at him in such a manner took the wind out of his sails when it came to asking how she felt. He justified his thinking by saying, *"If she needs something, she'll scream it at me."* A month into their research, Sally addressed the elephant in the room. "You don't know shit about women, do you, Neil." Sally one day asked sarcastically. Neil smiled. "Not a damn thing. You are my first serious relationship. Sally blushed. "Really, Neil? I had no idea. As handsome and intelligent as you are," Neil smiled. "Nope. I kept my nose in the books and my body in the mountains. All my free time was spent exploring the smokey mountains." He shared. Sally laughed. "Your parents must have been very concerned. Neil laughed. "They did mention it once or twice." He laughed, recollecting such events. His father would say things like. "Boy, I pray you don't bring home a dear for a wife." His Mother would join in, saying, "Winston, you know that boy prefers wolves." Sally frowned at hearing that. "Well, that was kind of cruel." She complained. "Nah, it was just my folk's way of telling me that there is more to life than work." Sally laughed. "Well, if they had just said that." She complained. "They did, in their way." Sally nodded. "I get it. My parents lacked your family's earthy dialogue, but my Mother and Father, both academics, insisted that I marry a highly educated man with good prospects." She reflected. Neil laughed. "Well, you screwed up getting married to me." Sally pushed him. "Why would you say such a thing." Neil shrugged. "Face it, sweetheart, I'm not going to have a line of people wanting to exchange their prosperity with the man who's come to tell them the world will end, and their money won't save them," Neil complained. "Listen, asshole, in case you haven't noticed, I'm pregnant, and my parents will love you because you're making them grandparents! Now stop upsetting me, and let's get ready to pack because I do not have my child in the swamps." Sally demanded. Stunned by the news, Neil asked. "Where do you want to go?" He asked stupidly. Take me home." She said abruptly. Neil smiled. "My home, not yours." She clarified. "Neil's smile turned into a frown. "I hate the cold," Neil whined. "Well, if what we've discovered is true, you might have to get over that." Sally pointed out.

Defiled

Terra wondered at the arrogance of humanity. Many, if not all, have forgotten or abandoned that they are of her. Perhaps it was a mistake to listen to Lucifer's advice about making their instincts so powerful, although, at the time, it did seem wise, as humans are born without fangs, claws, or fur. They were relatively slow compared to the rest of the animal kingdom. Their advantages came from potential. While the other animals were perfect, humans were not. They could, however, evolve, and that evolution came in the form of intelligence. Sadly, instead of getting to know his earthly home better, his fear, no doubt born through the cruelty of Nature, humans decided to separate themselves from her and developed organized religion, which insisted that Mankind was not a part of Nature but created by gods. Confusing the Grand Creator with a scaled-down version of a Creator. They then proceeded to respect less while expecting more. Terra reflected how early human history showed a more humble species. They would be in family units, taking only what they needed. She never wasted food and occasionally thanked Nature for all she provided. That was in the hunter-gatherer and early farming communities, but once they began creating cities, it seemed to Terra the time when Mankind lost its way. As cities grew larger, humans became more abusive in using natural resources. With this expansion, the need for resources grew while the supply slowly dwindled because early humans did not practice Conservationism on a large-scale basis. The lack of resources was an unprecedented invitation to war. Even though Humans had turned into a destructive force, it was still manageable until the industrial age. A harbinger of a terrifying future, the middle of the eighteenth century introduced the world to a new age that began on a tiny island Nation. As intoxicating as any drug and as communicable as the most contagious disease, this new age spread quickly around the world, and with it, a new level of waste, pollution, and poisons was being introduced to the eco-sphere. Terra recalled one of the rare moments when Gia spoke to Terra. It was a quiet evening, and Nature was doing what She did when the prompting came, *"Terra, daughter."* came the call. Terra stretched herself over the seas where her Mother's spirit resided. "I am here, Mother." She responded. The liquid voice spoke again. *"Daughter, what has happened? My waters are carrying a strange taste to them."* Gia observed. "Mother, humans have taken to the seas in monstrous ships energized by the remains of your earlier children. They call it oil, and it powers almost everything now." Terra explained. *This news is unsettling."* Gia responded." Terra smiled at her Mother's understatement. "It is indeed." Terra agreed. *"I shall not keep you from your duties, child,"* Gia said in preparation to depart. "But Mother, I will need your help in controlling the inspirations of these mortals." Terra began to realize. *"No, my daughter. You are never to interfere with their progress."* Gia reprimanded. "But Mother, what if they're going to destroy themselves?" Terra pursued. *"Then that will be their fate. Our mandate, given by the Infinite and Eternal, is to use the materials they've provided to begin a species that would evolve into a being that would eventually join, not enable them. They must advance or perish according to their desires."* Gia pointed out. Terra paused, and the realization set in. "So you're saying that other than a ghostly apparition of yourself, I must do this all alone? Terra could hear the liquid sigh. *"Daughter, the Creators sent you with me. Have faith that they will not abandon you and send you aid when you most need it."* Gia's voice faded as she returned to her rest in the Oceans of the world. Terra wondered about the help her Mother had spoken of. Where, from these greedy, selfish, fearful creatures, would one rise, separate himself from his contempt-filled brethren to join with her? She wondered. Terra observed herself and saw jets streak across the sky, spreading chemicals into her blue skies. She could hear birds complaining about how the sky had become crowded and very dirty. Her focus shifted, and she saw a volcano about to erupt; she quickly checked the vitals of the smoker and saw it would be minor. Terra knew the world was very close to a tipping point between all the pollutants in the air. A major volcanic eruption could have disastrous consequences. "Well," Terra pondered aloud. "According to Mother, I won't be alone in my time of need; I think no such help will come. I see these humans for what they are: frightened, unwilling to accept what is as opposed to what they wish to be. Unrealistic. Demanding, fearful, and selfish. How could the Creators ever think this species could join them in Glory? Is it possible that the Creators are more like the humans in their wishful thinking? Another thought struck Terra, which was more disconcerting than her precious thoughts. *"Have I become so tainted by having to contend with mankind?"* She wondered. The thought unsettled Terra; she vowed to be alert and open-minded. Little did Terra realize that the forces of Creation had already set the sequence of events needed for the laws of chance and probability to align to allow for the Dame and Sire of the Parental units that would give birth to them that would come to Nature's aid. The help will come in a form unexpected from a place of small repute. Battles growing in intensity came not from humanity but from the repercussions of unmindful actions. The long-discovered control of fire was a tale of warning unheeded in the great city of Chicago fire when a woman accidentally kicked over a kerosene lamp, and thousands were left homeless. She was drawn to the Sheffield flood, killing two hundred and forty people. Terra kept the flies and mosquito population down to avoid a plague. In the taming of an earthquake, she inadvertently saved the Life of a man who was the grandfather of the Man who would sire one of Terra's defenders. Terra worked harder than she thought she would ever have to, never dreaming that the Creators' visions would be so complex. Terra began to ponder if humans had to be the species the Creators were looking to join them. She began to wonder if she could lift another to take their place. Chimpanzees or even dolphins? They were both intelligent and suitable, she believed, as a replacement for the Creator's plan. The more Terra thought about it, the more likely it seemed. Perhaps I've been too narrow in my thinking. Chimps indeed show disturbing similarities in behavior that mirror humans. Both are hostile, but chimps are more vigorous, which makes them an easier target for corruption. Terra considered her alternatives. The advantages were that she could raise a more tranquil species that could live harmoniously with its environment. The disadvantage is time. How long would it take her to raise the intelligence of either species to be as technologically advanced as humanity? The disadvantage? What if Creation was looking at humanity as its chosen species? She would have failed her mandate. Worse yet, what if the newly chosen species turned out worse than humanity?! The thought shook Terra.

CHAPTER 6
Cold Births

It was a cold, blustery day in Minneapolis. The wind-driven snow created near-white-out conditions. "Just breathe, madam." The nurse could be heard saying. Diane Rogers looked at the nurse with venom in her eyes. "What the hell do you think I'm doing." She shouted in return. Understanding her predicament, the nurse smiled and nodded. "Where the hell is my husband?" Diane asked loudly. "He'll be right in, madam." The nurse replied. "Terry! Terry, get your ass in here!" Diane screamed. "I'm here, baby; I'm right here," Terry replied soothingly, rushing to stand beside his wife. "Look at what you did to me, you piece of shit!" She berated. Terry smiled. "You give us some healthy babies, and I'll spend the rest of my life making it up to you, darling," Terry promised. The doctors gently squeezed in between Terry and Diane. "Okay, Mrs. Rogers, are we ready?" Diane grabbed the Doctor. "Get these things out Now!" She demanded. A contraction caused Diane to scream. "Okay, bear down." Diane did as the Doctor ordered. It wasn't easy, but Diane gave birth to twins by the night's end. Lance and Ellie. Six pounds, eight ounces, bronze-skinned, and green eyes, the twins favored their Mother; in any case, Terry was ecstatic. The twins stared with sparkling green eyes at their father. A nurse handed the twins to Terry, who cradled and kissed them gently. Tears formed in his eyes. "I'm sorry we didn't bring you into a better world, my babies." He whispered gently. As if in answer, the wind increased. The weather had been changing dramatically over the last decade, and when Diane found out she was pregnant, she insisted on going home. While not a fan of the cold, Perry knew better than to argue with his stubborn wife, so they packed up the life they had begun, observing wildlife in the swamps of Florida and moved to the midwest. The past nine months have seen a severe shift in the weather pattern. It was one of the reasons they were in Florida. The state was suffering severe impacts from climate change. From hurricanes to flooding, ocean levels could rise on ocean shorelines everywhere. The entire world was feeling the effects. One evening, a pregnant Diane was watching the news with increasing dread. Terry came home from work drenched in sweat from the humid swamps to find his wife sitting on their bed with empty suitcases at her feet. "Hey, baby," Terry said softly while walking into his bedroom and seeing his wife. "Are you leaving me?" Terry asked nervously, unable to think of what he'd done to upset her. Diane looked up thoughtfully. "What? No, you idiot." She quipped. At that moment, she took in the scene of her sitting on the bed with unpacked suitcases. *"What else would he think?"* She asked herself. Diane stood and embraced her husband. "I'm sorry, Terry. I was sitting here watching the news and suddenly got an urge." She began.

"An urge for what?" Terry interjected. Diane looked Terry in the eyes. "To go." She responded. Terry grinned. "Okay, I'll bite. Go where?" He inquired. Diane's grin grew. "Home. I want to have the babies in my hometown." She replied. Terry frowned. Diane was feeling her husband get tense and held him tighter. "Baby, please, I'd feel much better, more comfortable." She reasoned. Terry shrugged. "What about our work?" He asked. Diane smiled. "Well, I thought it would be great if we started working on a reservation," Diane suggested. Terry's brows furrowed. "I'm sorry, what?" Terry asked, unsure he heard adequately. "You heard me. Listen, even as a child, I thought my effort would best be served to help our original citizens." Diane exclaimed defensively. Terry took a deep breath. "I see; so you want to give birth, raise our children, and work in Minnesota?" Terry asked, seeking clarification. "No, not necessarily,"

Diane claimed. "I thought you wanted to help Native Americans?" Terry countered, becoming confused. "Yes, my love, I do. I thought about The Black Foot reservation in Montana." She responded, waiting for a reaction. Terry walked to the bedroom window. "You won't miss out on the cold. The winters can be brutal out there." Terry mused. He began pacing the apartment while thinking aloud. "So, you want to go now, have the children in your hometown, then move to Montana? Terry concluded. Diane looked at her husband anxiously. "Yes, what do you think?" Diane asked. "Let me see if there might be any grants the University might be offering," Terry suggested. "If we're going to freeze, we might as well get paid for it." He joked. Diane smiled and hugged him tightly. "Genius! That's why I married you." She teased. He grinned in return. "Oh, you mean it wasn't the size of me," He began while his hand moved toward his pelvic region. She shoved him away. "Pig." She accused. "My thighs, the size of my thighs, what? You always said you thought I had sexy legs." Terry complained. Diane lowered her head. "You're nasty. Get on the phone and call the University; I will call some real estate agents and see what is available just off the reservation." Diane managed the incidentals as usual while Terry secured a grant for them to study the water tables and the natural food supply. Diane secured a small home in Santa Rita off King's Road. She had also called and arranged a meeting with the tribe elders to introduce herself and explain how she would like to help the community. It appeared to have gone well, as Diane seemed very optimistic about the conversation. After the twins were born, the family moved to the State of Montana, never imagining the reception that awaited them.

The family pulled up to their new home. It was a bright day. A slight chill to the air made things seem crisp and clean. Diane stepped out of the vehicle and took a deep lungful of air. She turned to smile at her husband, who returned the smile. A small welcoming committee met them. An Elder raised his hand in greeting. Terry approached the man and gave a slight bow. "Greetings, Father; we thank you for meeting us warmly," Terry uttered. The Elder smiled. "I am called John." The Elder responded. "I am Doctor Terry Rogers; this is my wife, Doctor Diane Rogers, and our twin children, Lance and Ellie." Terry introduced his family. John nodded to Diane as John introduced them, but all of the committee, especially the woman, laser-focused on the twins. They began to speak amongst themselves.

Terry looked at John. "What are they saying?" Terry asked. John gestured to a red building down the road from where the Rogers were staying. "If you would join us in the red square tonight, we will invite all of our elders; there is much we must explain to you." John invited. Terry looked at Diane, who nodded. "Of course, we can be there. I hope you don't mind that we bring the children." John raised his hand. "Of course, thank you." He turned, and he and the committee walked toward the red building John had earlier pointed out.

Inspiration

Terra felt overwhelmed. It seemed that another catastrophe was occurring elsewhere with every measure she took to restore order. The twentieth and twenty-first centuries were no laughing matter. It has always been a sad fact that Humanity used the planet as a toilet, but Nature could handle it, at least she WAS able to, once upon a time. A time when she didn't have Billions of people crawling on her back, discarding waste in a manner that did not accommodate the natural world. This lack of awareness has brought the world to calamity as food resources were dwindling. Water supplies were in danger of becoming too contaminated to sustain life, the air was becoming so noxious it required minimal toxicity to be rendered unbreathable, and Humanity still only made the smallest gestures to address the situation. It was no wonder that The Great Mother was beginning to fray at the edges. Nature, who masterfully followed the designs (as created by the forces of Creation.) for Humanity, saw the species in its innocence, and Nature thought she saw the reasoning behind the Creator's ambitions. A frail species with no fangs or claws, no fur to keep warm, and exposed to the elements, Nature marveled at Humanity's ingenuity and resilience. The crowning achievement was the species' sense of curiosity, adaptability, and analytical skills far beyond the other species. In all this wonder, Nature, who was no fool, was also tempted by the forces of Chaos to abandon her mandate, as Humanity now seemed to be doing. With Chaos so firmly embedded in Humanity's thinking, how is Nature supposed to convince them that all the achievements they have gained in the past millennium are destructive to them when their comparison involved a period in history when they died much younger? With modern Technology, they live more comfortably and for longer than ever! Why would they give anything up if all they saw or wanted to see were the advancements? Forget the millions dead from war or the people starving or rampant sickness in what more technologically advanced countries are now calling the third world as if there was a separate world! Terra was so dejected she acted inconducive to the continued maintenance of the environment. Heat waves, cold snaps, rogue waves, earthquakes, bug infestations. Terra was striking back in a fury, but Humanity ignored the signs, convinced their Technology would save them. They (Humanity) have gone as far as making a business off the works of the Creator. Selling forgiveness and good fortune under the name of Capitalism. Terra became deeply depressed when she believed that the work of her Mother, herself, and the Creator would be for nothing because Terra believed that Humanity was unworthy. One sunrise, Terra stood on the Ocean crying. She was formulating a plan to destroy the world. Dolphins, Whales, and squids surrounded her, speaking for the world's marine life; they pled with her. "Mother. We were the first life that took in air, and now you think to remove that which you so freely gave?" They cried out in their clicks and vocalizations. Terra looked sadly at them. "I am sorry, my children, but this world was designed as a cradle for humanity to grow in, but instead of growing, they have embraced destruction as a form of self-expression." She observed. The brightest of the Marine life, The dolphins, whales, and squids, put up a robust debate. "Does it have to be Humanity?" The dolphin clicked. "Yes." Argued the Whale. "There are many among us that are brighter than humans." The Whale pointed out. Terra nodded in agreement. "Undoubtedly." Terra nodded. "I knew many, but it is not my plan; the Creator desires it be Humanity. The Marine life did not react well. The dolphins jumped out of the water, flipping while the whales did massive belly flops, and the squids looked at Terra accusingly. "You do realize this is not appreciated at all." The squid pointed out. Terra bowed her head dejected. "I'd imagine not, but what can I do? The only way I can interact with humans is through Nature. I cannot speak to them directly." A whale interjected. "Why not?" The Whale asked. Nature grinned. "Because that would prove the existence of external influences." Terra responded. "It's not like they don't believe in those things already." A dolphin clicked. "Yes," Nature responded, but it's only that, a belief. If they knew, well, if they knew the Creator knows, Their response would lead to their destruction as demands were made by immature minds that could not fathom the consequences, which is why they have to go through the growth stage but their incessant demands have become dangerous to himself and his environment. "Yes, Mother, but what you propose would end everything! I cannot believe this was all created to rest upon the whims of a self-loathing species! The Makers must have a contingency plan, or they saw into the future and saw humankind achieve the heights set for him." A dolphin argued. "All of what is said is argumentative because if the Creator does not send me aid soon, I see no alternative but to…" Nature became silent, as did all the Marine life gathered around her. "It would seem as if Gia has something to share." They observed. The water seemed alive as The Mother, Gia, spoke through the waves. *"Daughter, you have been heard by the Creators, and you have been sent aid. Two shall come to you soon to offer the help you sought. They are modeled after the Creators and shall wield power. They shall be your children. Utilize them well, for much was taken from the Infinite to form these two. They shall be ambassadors for you. Through them, let your desires be revealed to Humanity. The only thing not to be shared is the divine plan for the human race. If they were to discover their destiny, the knowledge would corrupt them, and all would be lost. Pay heed for their coming."* The Great Mothers' voice trailed off, receding with the waves. Terra stood with tears of joy trickling down her cheeks. "Finally!" Terra rejoiced. Perhaps now her voice will be known. Nature never enjoyed being ostracized by those she considered her children. She could never have fathomed that taking Satan's recommendation of utilizing fear as their most powerful stimuli would make the conversion to enlightenment exponentially difficult. With her new disciples, she can not only enforce her will but, through her emissaries, let Humanity know the harmful effects their meddling with the natural order of things is having. Terra spat as the taste of vile chemicals filled her mouth, and she knew the Humans were doing it again. Nature flashed over to where she knew the toxic spillage to be. The Cuyahoga River, Cleveland, Ohio, America. A spark from a dock worker's torch touched the water, causing the river to burst into flames. Unseen, Nature aided in the fight to extinguish the blaze by creating small whirlpools that kept the fire contained. Sadly, more chemicals were used to put the fire out. There was so much pollution that despite Terra's efforts to disperse the pollution, the river caught fire numerous times. Looking deeper into her Mother's place of retirement, Terra was appalled. She realized that humanity must go insane when she witnessed the unthinkable. This selfish, undisciplined species had created what they dubbed "The Great Pacific Patch." This patch is a concentration of plastic debris, including micro-plastics, that is harmful to marine life. Perhaps the deadliest of these micro-plastics are called "Nurdles." Tiny plastic pellets floating in the Ocean cause as much damage as oil spills but are, as of yet, considered hazardous. This garbage island encompasses an area that covers one point six million square kilometers! Twice the size of Texas in the U.S. or three times that of France." Upon discovering the tiny patch, Nature believed that Humanity would clean it up when they discovered it. What Nature discovered about her ward species was that they wouldn't if Humanity did not have to do something. The sadness became the complacency of Humanity. Terra once asked her Mother, the great Gia spirit, if it was possible that because Humanity no longer had predators to fear, they began to predate among themselves, becoming both predator and prey?" Gia ruminated over the query for a century before responding. "Daughter. You made an astute observation; I am content to say that you will probably learn that answer before I do." Gia teased. Terra was no closer to confirmation a millennium later, although her speculation agreed. Aiding as much as she could, Nature found it becoming increasingly difficult to do her work effectively as the mechanisms of Nature began to react to Humanities interference. Weather patterns were beginning to shift as climate change became a more viable force to contend with. Terra was fighting many wars on many fronts as Humanity, as a collective, decided that the problems they created for themselves would somehow disappear. Of course, Nature saw Technology as a large contributor to the issue. With it, Humanity has seen deep into the cosmos. Extended their lifespans (Although it could be argued that simple hygiene could have been a a significant contributor to that particular fact. Humans somehow made things better and yet worse than they had ever been. Humanity has made enormous cities for their people to live in. The trade-off. The millions upon millions of trees that were slain. The grass and underbrush were razed so that neat lawns could be planted, the air so dirty the stars could barely be seen anymore. The air is barely breathable, and the water becomes undrinkable. Humans have created chemicals they refer to as "Forever chemicals."

CHAPTER 7

Discovery

The tribe elders told Diane that her children had gifts; when asked what sort of gifts, they said Lance was a "Nikoskoa." to the Earth, and Ellie was the Nokomis or spirit of the Earth goddess. When Diane asked them how that made her children special, they only smiled with a look of reverence. When Diane told Terry about it, he smiled. "Honey, you know how the Native American revere children." He responded dismissively. Diane was not as dismissive; her gut told her there was much more to it than mere reverence. One day, the twins were out with their Parents, and while Diane was taking water samples from a nearby lake, Ellie ran off into the woods to explore. While most parents wouldn't allow their children to run off unsupervised, Lance and Ellie possessed the fiercely independent will and did as they wished while maintaining respect and courtesy.

Since they had the protection of the Blackfoot nation, both Diane and Terry were comfortable with letting them explore as they chose as long as they shared where they would be going. One particularly hazy day, Diane found Ellie crouching down. Diane stared in disbelief as she listened to her daughter speak to a dear who was drinking calmly from a pond.

"That water looks very refreshing," Ellie said softly to the dear. The animal slowly raised its head from sipping, licked its lips, and took a few steps back from the pond. Ellie, who was squatting a few yards away, slowly stood up. Usually, most deer would run at such an action, but the dear stood in place, and much to Diane's astonishment, she watched as her daughter rose, slowly walked beside the dear, kneeled beside the pond, and sipped! Finishing her drink, Ellie looked up at the deer, who nuzzled Ellie before turning and scampering off into the woods. Ellie raised her head as she heard sobbing. Getting up, Ellie walked over to the spot the sound was coming from. Ellie was surprised to see her Mother sitting on the ground crying. "Mom? Mom, are you okay?" Ellie inquired, deeply concerned. Diane jumped to her feet and hugged her daughter. Ellie melted in her arms. "Are you okay, Mom?" Ellie asked. Diane smiled, wiping tears. "Yes, baby." She responded. "I'm very okay," Diane replied with a grin. The two held hands as they walked back to a couple of horses they had tied to a tree. The sun had passed the midday point. They mounted the steeds and began the ride home.

Ellie sang about nesting birds, amusing her Mother. "Where did you learn that song, sweetheart?" Diane probed. "The birds taught me." Was Ellie's simple reply. Diane, who was leading, slowed her mount so Ellie could ride beside her. "When, baby? When did the birds teach you?" Diane asked curiously. Ellie looked up at her Mother with a smile. "Every morning, Mom. They wake me up asking me to come out and play." Diane was astounded that her daughter was growing so fast right before her eyes. "Baby, you know not to tell anyone of the gifts you have?" Diane cautiously asked. "Why not, Mom?" Ellie asked innocently. Diane expressed a sigh before her explanation. "Baby, most people would not understand or even believe you have extraordinary abilities." Ellie looked confused. "What gifts, Mom?" The response was extended as Diane tried thinking of how to explain to her daughter that the Nature of humanity was one of envy and jealousy.

"Baby, no one can do what you do." Diane expressed plainly. Ellie stopped her horse. Diane looked back at her. "Sweetie?" She said she was concerned that she might have given her daughter information her young mind was unprepared for. "No one hears the birds?" Ellie asked sadly. Diane reached out to touch Ellie's hand. "Baby, we hear them, but they don't speak to us like they do to you." A distraught Diane explained. "What does it sound like to you?" The young girl inquired. Diane thought of the best way to describe it. "It sounds like very pretty whistling." She explained. Ellie smiled. "Yes. I hear that too, but inside the whistles, I hear words." Diane smiled. "That is part of your gift," Diane responded. Ellie thought about it for a moment. "Do I have other gifts?" That was the next question. Diane laughed joyfully. "Well, according to Alsoome, you are the Nokomis, something that will make itself known to you as you get older," Diane explained. "But Mom." Ellie began. "Enough questions; let us focus on getting home. The light won't last long." Diane deflected, knowing her curious daughter would ask questions she did not have answers to.

Nikoskoa

Terry was staring at what looked like a mound a short distance away. "What's up pop?" Lance asked his father as he came up behind him. Terry pointed ahead. "What's that?" He asked. Lance squinted where his father pointed. Lance, who had incredible vision, looked back at his father. "It looks like a den to me." At fourteen years old, Lance and his sister were incredibly mature and, with the aid of the Blackfoot tribe, raised their children to have a profound love of all things natural. "I can see it's a den boy; just wondering what animal." Terry clarified. Lance inched forward to get a better look. "Lance!" Terry called for his son to be careful. Lance looked back. "Looks like a big cat. Mountain lion or something." Lance whispered. Terry signaled for them to leave. Exploding from the den, a mountain lion, who had been watching them since they entered the area, charged them. Terry jumped in front of Lance. The charging cat ran into him, slamming him to the ground, but before the cat could do any harm, Lance yanked on its tail, causing the lion to spin and face Lance, who was slowly backing into the cat's den. The mountain lion roared mightily. Lance changed direction, leaving a path for the great cat to approach the den unmolested. Slowly, he walked to his father, who had gotten up while rubbing where the cat had rammed into him. The cat had walked up to the mound and quickly stuck his head into the entry pulled his head out and stared at Lance with a low growl. Lance approached his father and gently took his hand. "Let's go, Dad." Lance directed. "What?" Terry asked. "Turn around, and let's go," Lance repeated. "You want to turn our backs on a man-eater?" Terry asked, surprised. "She's not hungry, Dad," Lance observed. Terry tilted his head. "Oh, and what is she then?" Terry posed. "A new Mom," Lance answered. Looking at his father, who was wide-eyed in awe when, as predicted by his son, the lion, no longer feeling threatened, crawled into her den, allowing the trespassers to leave unmolested. "Son, that was amazing." Terry blurted. Lance smiled. "I'm not sure why you're so surprised; it's how you, Mom, and the Blackfoot people taught us everything we know." Lance pointed out. Terry shook his head. "That might be so, but the Blackfoot also told us when you were very young that there is something special about you two." Terry pointed out. Lance waved away the compliment. "Give me a moment, Dad." Lance requested. Terry looked at his son. "Okay, but what's up?" He inquired. Lance smiled. "Just helping a single mom." Lance half-joked. Lance walked away in a predator's stalk; a moment later, Terry heard scrambling in nearby bushes, and Lance came out with a freshly killed rabbit. Lance walked past his father toward the lion's den. Lance whispered into the den, dropped the rabbit in front of it, and then walked back to his father, who watched his son's actions with immense pride. "Let's get back home," Terry suggested. Lance nodded. "Dad, what's going on?" Lance inquired. "Regarding what, son?" Terry asked, unsure where his son was taking the inquiry. "You won't let us watch television, but I've noticed a few things," Lance admitted. Terry smiled. Since he began to talk, Lance has always shown concern about things he had little information about. "Not sure what you're getting at, son," Terry admitted. "I can see it, Dad," Lance said directly. "What is it that you see, son?" Terry inquired, trying to conceal his nervousness. Lance stared at his father. "Ellie and I can handle whatever you need to tell us." Lance pointed out. Terry smiled and patted his son on the back. "No worries, son." Terry tried to placate his son. Unconvinced with his father's explanation, Lance would speak to the Alsoome, who knew the knowledge Lance and his Sister would need. Lance was anxious as he began having violent dreams of war and sickness. Lance tried to hide his anxiety from his father. Lance knew he had to speak with Ellie. He realized that their growth had been somehow accelerated and that they would be involved in momentous events, but the when, where, and why were still a mystery that haunted him. Lance wondered if his Mother and Sister arrived home yet. Looking at his father, he saw a look of deep concern. Lance knew that whatever the reason, he would make this man proud. His father was a warrior in his own right and battled many ignorant people who tried to silence him and his Mother for the notions they taught. They disclaimed Terry's Father as a woodsman with no proper scholastic background and that his Mother was a sentimentalist and had not published any significant papers establishing significant bona fides. They were listed as local agitators and were harmless. But as Winston would say. "Don't discount the gun that hasn't chambered a round." His round-about way of equating Terry as the chambered round. As it became apparent what the major corporations were doing and the direction society and the environment was taking, his Mother and Father were at the forefront with the "Protect the Earth Foundation," they had started and tried to warn the Governments of the world what their research had revealed. They were re-soundly rejected. They were labeled alarmists and extremists. The industrialized world's major corporations so disliked them that a misinformation campaign was launched to ridicule their findings. They mocked the idea that the Earth was a living entity. Made ridiculous claims that pollution was manageable and recycling was doing its designed function. The newest and most disturbing to Terry was the ineffectual agencies developed to oversee the pollution-makers. The P.P.A. is responsible for the purchase of renewable energy. The C.A.A., the Clean Air Act. The E.P.CR.A. is responsible for informing the public in case of the toxic release of chemicals. The C.W.A. is responsible for safeguarding the nation's water supply and prohibiting the discharge of pollutants. The F.I.F.R.A. is in charge of regulating, along with The E.P.A., who, combined, is in charge of pesticides and provides guidelines for distribution. They may be the most ineffectual or compromised agencies, as America's major contributor to pollution is the use of pesticides and farmland runoff into our water supply. Terry and his wife feared for their children, for although they possessed a power that seemed growing and fought for a just cause, the twins would be fighting the entire industrialized world. No one would surrender their comforts or what they think to be their rewards for years of research, effort, and, most importantly, a profit that is their just due. Regardless, it seems, of the consequences. It was decided long ago that the wealthy and the powerful would do whatever it took to stay in the position they've carved out of people's selfishness and desire for possessions. Yes, Terry realized that for all the faults placed upon the Wealthy for the position Mankind found itself in, it was the backing of people experiencing poverty, the spending whatever was of value to purchase the materials or services being provided. For comfort and convenience. Enabling a sedentary lifestyle as a measurement of success alongside possessions caught the eye and stirred envy and jealousy. These actions and reactions were also to blame for the Earth's condition. *"What will Diane do when the twins go to battle?"* Terry wondered for the thousandth time. While Diane was no wilting flower, like most Mothers, she was very protective of their children. Terry sighed. "That's a bridge I'll cross when I get there. "Dad?" Lance whispered. Shaken from thinking, Terry looked at his quickly maturing son and smiled. "What's up, kid." Terry responded nonchalantly. Lance cocked his head. "Funny, I was about to ask you the same thing." Lance retorted. Terry squinted, pretending to be confused. Lance tilted his head to the other side, reminding Terry of a curious bird. "You had that. I'm on an astral journey. Look in your eyes, and I wondered why you were so engaged that you didn't answer any of my questions." Lance pointed out. Terry looked surprised. "Did I do that?" He inquired seriously. Lance nodded. "You did, and it was a bit unnerving." Terry shook his head. "I apologize for that, Lance, and yes, my thoughts were elsewhere. He explained. Lance stood quietly for a moment. The moment passed, and Lance probed. "And?" He pushed. "And what?" Terry redirected. Lance sighed loudly. Terry peered at his son, blinking slowly. "Dad." Lance insisted. "Lance!" Terry shot back. Lance stopped walking and crossed his arms. "You do remember I am the Nikoskoa." Lance demanded. Terry stared at his son. "You do remember I am your Father!" Terry responded. "But how will I learn if you withhold information from me?" Lance pled. Terry smiled and put his arm around Lance's shoulder. "What ran through my head were Mom and Dad's concerns, not yours or your Sisters, understand?" Terry explained. Mollified, Lance nodded. "Okay, Pop."

CHAPTER 8
Terra Strikes

It was a scorching and humid day in the Cordoba region of the beautiful country of Spain. The sky was cloudless, promising an excellent day. Manuel was finishing his packing when he called out to his cousin Hector. "Primo, you done packing?" He called out. His excited cousin responded. "Pendeho, I'm at the door waiting for you," Hector replied sarcastically. "Really?" Manuel answered with equal sarcasm. "Did you call the girls?" The only response to Manuel's query was a moment of silence followed by Hector banging into the table as he scrambled to make the call. "I guess not, puto." Manuel laughed. Moments later, Manuel heard his cousin. "Hey, it's Hector. I'm calling to ask if you are ready yet?" Hector inquired. "Mijo, we've been sitting here waiting on you guys. A sexy voice complained. "I'm sorry, Lisa, but we overslept. Apologize to Dalia; we're on our way." Hector promised. "You better be." Lisa retorted. Hector turned to find Manuel behind him. "Well?" He asked. "Well, what?" Hector demanded. "Are they ready?" Manuel demanded. "Yeah," Hector replied. "And now you got Lisa pissed off at me," Hector complained. "No, senor, she's acting pissed off because she is spoiled, and you like to spoil her." Manuel pointed out. "Whatever, man, can we go?"

Hector pled. The men drove to their companion's home, and Hector complained about being late. When they got there, they quickly packed their Gear while Lisa complained. In the car, Manuel turned the music on loudly. "Why is the music so loud?" Lisa complained. "I'll lower it if you stop bitchin'," Manuel muttered. "What did you say?" Lisa complained. "Nothing," Manuel said softly. "I thought so." Lisa retaliated. Manuel drove to the Parque Natural, Sierra y Montoro. "What took you guys so long? I thought we were going to start early; what happened? Do you know how hot it will be when we get there?" Lisa incessantly complained. "Madre de Dios, give it a rest Lisa. We overslept; that's all there is to it." Manuel complained. Lisa looked at Hector. "I know you won't let him speak to me that way." She complained. Hector smiled crookedly. "Lisa, we came out to be in the fresh air and enjoy some of what's left of Nature; why all the drama?" Hector begged. Lisa huffed and fell to mumbling to herself. "I didn't want to go on this stupid trip anyway." Lisa huffed. Manuel sighed. "Why did you agree then?" He asked. "Why do you think? Because Dalia asked me to." Lisa complained. "I invited you." Dalia clarified. Lisa turned on Dalia. "Oh, you too? You get to acting funny when you get around Manny." Lisa complained. Hector squeezed Lisa's hand. "Ja." He said softly. "Enough? Enough what?" Lisa insisted. "Enough acting like a spoiled child," Hector demanded. Lisa fell silent, and the rest of the drive was filled with music from the radio. Arriving at the National Park, the beauty of it put even Lisa in better spirits. "It is beautiful," Dalia observed. Manuel took a deep breath. "Smells good." He said while smiling. "Okay, we ready?" he asked. Hector looked at Lisa's feet. "Baby, what are you wearing?" Lisa looked down at her feet. "What?" She asked defensively. "You did understand that we were going to a National park?" Manuel inquired. "Of course, I knew stupid." She reacted angrily. Hector sighed, knowing where this was going to lead. "If you knew, why are you wearing fuck me spiked heels on a hiking trip?" Manuel exclaimed. "C'mon bro, you don't gotta talk to her like that," Hector complained. Manuel slowly looked at his cousin. "Seriously, Hector?" Manuel asked. "Yo, guys," Dalia called. "This is some bullshit, Manny. Can we please go hiking? Let her wear whatever the fuck she wants to wear." Dalia bitterly complained. "I know you don't like Lisa, but," Hector piped in defense of Lisa. Manuel interjected. "Primo, it's not that I don't like her." Hector threw his hands up. "What then?" He asked flabbergasted. Manuel rolled his eyes. "C'mon, bro, she always wants things her way; she always makes things harder than they need to be." Manuel pointed out. "Guys!" Dalia shouted. Both men fell silent as Dalia seldom raised her voice. Hector and Manuel turned to see Dalia pointing to Lisa's retreating as she walked down a path into the woods. Hector called out to her. "Lisa, baby, where are you going?" Hector shouted. "You wanted to walk in the fucking woods. Well, let's go." She shouted. Manuel looked at Hector. "I brought some moccasins. You might want to bring them." He suggested. Hector cocked his head to the side in a gesture of miscomprehension. "I',m not trying to be a smart ass; it's just that within half a mile, she won't be able to walk anymore." Manuel pointed out. Hector rifled through his cousin's pack until he found the moccasins. "Thanks, primo," Hector muttered quietly. Manuel smiled. "Hey, you're my cousin; if you love crazy, I guess I gotta love her too." Hector grinned. "That's only a little funny." He cracked. "You know that's my friend, right?" Dalia complained.

A high-pitched scream rang through the woods. Hector cried out, "Lisa!" He ran off in the direction she had last seen going. Rounding a bend, Hector skidded to a stop when he heard sobbing. In a state of near hysteria, Hector shouted. "Lisa! Baby, where are you? At that moment, Manuel, accompanied by Dalia, rounded the bend. "Where is she?" Dalia asked. Hector was looking around wildly. "I don't know. She's gotta be around here somewhere." Hector insisted. "It's like she just disappeared," Manuel whispered. Hector was looking through the bushes. "No, she's here somewhere." He insisted. "How do you know that?" Manuel probed. Hector looked at his cousin. "I heard crying, and it came from close by." He demanded. Manuel nodded. "Okay, let's keep looking for her." He agreed. "Lisa, Lisa. Lisa came out. Stop playing games. This shit isn't funny anymore." Dalia complained. Hector glared at Dalia. "How do you know she's playing? She could be seriously hurt." Hector argued defensively. "I'm not trying to think of her hurt, okay? She's my friend; I know her; she likes to play." Dalia insisted as she began to cry. Manuel hugged her. "Don't worry, we'll find her." He assured her. Dalia hugged Manuel tightly. "You promise?" She begged. Manuel smiled. "Promise."

Spanish grass

Lisa walked away from her friends and cussed to herself. rounding a bend, she looked for another path into the woods, trying to avoid her friends. She was furious at Hector for not taking her side. Getting tired, she stopped to rest; slipping her shoes off, she felt the cool grass under her feet. A bug crawled on her leg, and much to her surprise, the bug seemed to be studying her as much as she was studying it. The bug seemed to rear on its hind legs and plunged its mandibles into her skin, causing her to jump in pain. "Maldito bicho!" She exclaimed while rubbing at the sight. She sat on a log, massaging the bitten area; in the background, she could hear her friends calling out to her. "Lisa, Lisa." They shouted. Lisa smiled at her friend's confusion. Becoming drowsy, she smiled to herself, thinking her friend's day would be spoiled if she kept quiet. The spiteful girl never felt the grass as it slowly entwined around her ankles. Coming out of a stupor, Lisa found tree limbs encircling her wrists and hoisting her into the air. Lisa screamed! a blood-curdling scream that echoed off the mountains. Moments later, her friends came around a bend to find Lisa hanging in the air, held by tree limbs that seemed to be slowly pulling her in a manner the body was not meant to be pulled. Screaming in excruciating pain, Lisa sobbed. "Please help me." She cried. Hector was in a state of near panic. Manuel reached for one of Lisa's legs, and the tree pulled harder, sending a new wave of pain through Lisa, who screamed again. "Stop pendeho. Don't you see you're hurting her?" Hector complained. "I'm not the one hurting her." Manuel replied. "It's that fucking tree." He argued in disbelief. "Hector," Lisa whined. "Please, papa, get me down from here." She begged, sounding exhausted. "Don't worry, baby; I'm gonna get you down." Hector promised as he scanned the woods for something that would help him. Dalia stood staring at her dangling friend. Lisa stared at her friend. "You did this to me, perra." Lisa accused. "If it wasn't for you and your need to impress your man," She trailed off as the limb holding her neck tightened. "Your fault." Lisa squeaked. Manuel Looked at Hector. "I got an ax in the trunk of the car." He remembered. "That's like a mile back." Hector complained. Manuel shrugged. "Give me the keys." Hector shouted. Manuel threw him his keys, and Hector ran down the path to the car. Dalia looked at

Manuel. "Manny, please help my friend." She pled. "We're doing what we can; when Hector returns, we'll chop this tree down and save your friend." Manuel tried to console Dalia. Strangely, when Manuel spoke of chopping the tree down, the wind picked up, sending leaves and debris into the faces of Manuel and Dalia. fifteen minutes later, an exhausted Hector approached the bend with an ax. Lisa moaned. "Baby, you came back for me." She cried. "I'm here, baby." Hector shouted, brandishing the ax. While she was hanging, the tree appeared drooping, but as soon as Hector came near it with the ax, it seemed to straighten up, yanking Lisa higher into the air and tightening its grip on her. Hearing her choke, Hector charged the tree, lifting the ax and preparing a powerful blow. The tree responded by tightening its grip to where Lisa's eyes bulged, and she gasped for breath. Manuel noticed what was happening and tried to calm his cousin down, but Hector, in desperation, shrugged him off and ran at the tree prepared to chop. Lisa's bone-chilling scream stopped Hector in his tracks as the tree seemed to rear up, loosening its grip for a moment; that was when Lisa screamed. In utter helplessness and fear, Dalia, Manuel, and Hector watched in horror as the impossible occurred and the tree, holding their friend prisoner, pulled on her until she could Stretch no more, and Lisa was ripped apart by the tree, showering them in blood and sending Lisa's head, arms and legs thrown in different directions causing Dalia to faint and Manuel to throw up while Hector fell to his knee's crying. Manuel wiped his mouth and realized they were still in danger. Shaking Dalia, Manuel screamed. "We gotta get the fuck out of here now." Dalia looked up, choking on her tears. "But Lisa." She wailed. Manuel turned in frustration to his cousin, who was on his knees crying. "Ah, mi amor, mi amor." Hector cried repeatedly. "Vamanos Hector." Manuel shouted at his unheeding cousin. Manuel stood in front of his cousin. "Primo!" Manuel shouted. His cousin continued to ignore him until Manuel raised his hand in an attempt to smack Hector into action, but instead, Manuel found his hand bound by a vine. Attempting to turn to look at what held him, he found his feet were bound by grass. Frightened, Manuel called his friends to aid him. Dalia kept her head down, refusing to look up, repeating to herself, "No, no, no, no, this aint happening." Seeing what was happening to his cousin, Hector inexplicably began to giggle. "Aww, she got you now." Manuel looked at Hector in shock. "Hec, ayudame." Manuel pled. At that moment, the ground seemed to open and swallow whole, a screaming Manuel Ortiz. Hector stared as the Earth took his cousin. "Ohh, looks like you've been snatched." Hector giggled maniacally. After a silence that lasted a few minutes, Hector finally stirred and looked up to where his woman was torn like a rag doll and to the floor where his cousin stood; remembering Dalia, he looked back to where he last remembered seeing her. A small mound stood where Dalia stood. Hector slowly made his way to the mound. He began inspecting it. He tore at the grass until, in near panic, he fell back, scrambled to his feet, and tore at more grass until Dalia's bloated, partially eaten face stared back at him with lifeless eyes. Hector slowly got to his feet, looked around, turned, and ran up the path they had come down from in absolute terror. Hector was found walking down the road that led to the park. He told his story to strangers visiting the park. In disbelief, they listened to his story about how the Earth swallowed his cousin, how his girlfriend was ripped into pieces, and how his cousin's girlfriend was smothered and half-eaten by only god knows what. The strangers brought Hector to the Park ranger's office, who promptly detained him until the police arrived. The evening news barely touched on the story and blamed Hector for luring his friends to the park where he murdered them. No further investigations were launched as the police thought they had an open and shut case. Hector refused to be quiet regarding his friend's death and claimed to anyone who would listen that the Earth had come to life and strangled and beheaded his woman, buried his cousin, and buried his cousin's girlfriend alive! He went on to say that he thought the Earth was on the warpath. Which, of course, was met with ridicule and a guilty verdict in his trial.

CHAPTER 9
Lost and Found

The Elders gathered in the community hall as was requested by the tribal Chief. Terry and Diane entered, found a place to sit, and waited while the rest of the town gathered. The Elder, who introduced himself as John, took to the podium. "Kwe." He said in greeting. My brothers and sisters, I greet you in harmony and wish our new neighbors welcome. Turning to Terry and Diane, giving a short bow. "Anamikagage, welcome. We thank you for making yourselves available for our questioning." John espoused. Terry stood. "We should thank you for such a warm reception," Terry said gratefully. "Why are you here?" John asked candidly. Not taken aback by his forthrightness, Terry repaid it by being equally direct. "My wife and I are conservationists and meteorologists, Doctors of the Earth. Before our babies were given to us by the Great Mother, we worked in the south measuring everything from air quality to bacteria production." Terry explained. "For what purpose?" John inquired. Diane stood beside her husband and held his hand, a gesture that did not escape the elders. "My husband and I have noticed that the Mother of all is ill. Her skies, water, and Earth have absorbed our greed and sickness." Diane complained. "The elders nodded. "We, too, have noticed. The Mother is sick, but not us made her so." John exclaimed. "We know that sir," Terry interjected. "We only see that she is. My wife and I have brought our children here to your land to help study the sickness and search for a cure." He exclaimed. "What kind of bullshit are you trying to sell?" A young man stood shouting and receiving a cheer from the younger members. Terry breathed deeply. "I understand the distrust you feel, but I have never lied to you nor broken any promises; I also cannot speak on what the government has done to you and all the tribes of this land. I can only speak for myself and my family; I am Terry Rogers. Adopted son of Winston and Sheryl, husband to Diane Silver-Rogers, Father to Lance and Ellie. We are here because your people have more of a connection with the Mother than we ever had and hope to add your knowledge to ours to find a cure to what ails her." Terry concluded. John stood. "You spoke well, son of Winston. We of the black foot nation accept your offer of aid, for we, too, have noticed the Mother's ailment. We will do what is in our power; you will have our protection and cooperation. You will serve us in helping the Mother of all recuperate. I, John, spotted the owl of the Siksika, so claims." The noble leader promised. Terry bowed." Thank you, sir. Do you have any questions for us?" Diane inquired. An older woman stood up and shuffled over to Diane and the children. Diane stood with both babies; the older woman began to inspect Ellie and Lance. The woman sniffed the baby's feet, peered intensely into both eyes and smelled their breath. She then mumbled in Lance's ear. His eyes widened, and to Terry and Diane's surprise, Lance laughed hysterically. Diane looked at Lance, deeply concerned. The Elder looked at Diane, smiled, and shook her head. For whatever reason, Diane understood that as a message: "Don't worry." Diane appeared to relax. The older woman then leaned close to Ellie's ear and whispered. Much to Diane's chagrin, Ellie's response was the opposite of her brothers. Where Lance laughed hysterically, Ellie wept. Her green eyes sparkled with tears; those tears turned into streams as they flowed down the pretty girl's face. Diane looked to the older woman, who (much to Diane and Terry's shock) found the Elder on her knees before Ellie and was followed by the rest of the council. Terry looked to John for clarification. Slowly rising, John looked at Terry and Diane, smiling. "We recognize the blessings our great Mother has graced our children with." John intoned solemnly. The implication did not escape Diane. "What do you mean by Our children?" Diane inquired, hoping her tone did not carry her anxiety. Looking at Diane sadly, John explained. "We see in the babies the great warden of the forest, and she that would speak for the great Mother. Do you now understand why I said our children?" John both explained and inquired. Diane stared at the elder Chief and slowly nodded. "Understand that no mother wishes to hear that her child is not her own and to predict with such certainty that one's children will soon no longer be theirs is…" Diane trailed off, close to tears. John spoke in tender tones. "It is not us who wish to separate you from the children, but we spoke a riddle to Lance, who found it amusing; to us, this spoke of the joy of life and its beauty. To Ellie, we spoke of wilting flowers and falling leaves, and her response spoke of the sadness Nature must endure as her colder aspects spoke of the silencing of her songs, which caused Ellie to cry, showing us she was in harmony with the Mother's vibrations." John proclaimed. Diane looked blankly at John. "I understand the words but not the meaning," Diane confessed. John bowed. "Your time and work with us shall clarify everything." John iterated. Terry extended his hand to the Chief; John clasped Terry's forearm. "You are family among us, and we thank you for blessing us with the care of these twins," John exclaimed. Terry grasped the forearm tightly. "We do not pretend to understand your ways, but if you would be patient with us," John raised his hand, interjecting. "Please, brother, You and your wife have much to do raising the children and your work; our ways will become familiar to you as you live among us; please do not concern yourself with our ways; they will soon become your ways." John consoled. Terry nodded. "We will follow your advice, John." Terry agreed. John smiled and turned to the assembly. "Brothers and sisters. Thank you for your time, patience, and understanding; we will gather again soon; go in peace." John said dismissively.

Decisions

Diane and Terry walked back to their new home. "What do you think?" She inquired. Terry appeared reflective. "I think we couldn't have asked for a warmer reception." He stated. Diane frowned. "Warm? Perhaps the proclamation that the twins were somehow more than anything but children was disconcerting." Diane admitted. Terry nodded. "That's understandable, honey, but we knew there was a reason we came here." Terry pointed out. "Yes." Diane agreed. "To learn about nature from a people very close to her, Not, I repeat, Not be told our children are more than they seem, or that by their sensitivities, our children have become public domain." She emphatically stated. A stray dog ran up and began barking at them as they approached their home. Terry placed himself between the dog and his family. At that moment, Lance woke up, rubbed the sleep out of his eyes, looked the dog in the eyes, and grunted. This was followed by a series of what Terry thought to be baby gibberish, but to Terry's and Diane's astonishment, the dog stopped barking and sat as if listening. The cherry on top was when a pack of stray dogs came from various directions, sitting beside the first dog as if to listen to the gibberish Lance spewed. Staring at his attentive audience, he finished with an authoritative "Ahh, nah na." In utter disbelief. The Rogers watched as the strays stood as one and went about their business in an orderly fashion. Terry and Diane stood in bewilderment and shock. "Okay," Terry muttered. "I need a drink." Diane nodded in agreement. Lance went back to sleep. Rummaging through yet unpacked boxes, Terry muttered. "I know it's in here somewhere." Putting the twins down to rest, Diane snuck up behind Terry, who was laser-focused on his search. "Hey." Diane whispered in his ear. Terry's head snapped up, banging his head. He rubbed his head rapidly and looked at Diane accusingly. Diane fought the impulse to laugh. Aww, sweetheart, are you okay?" Diane asked, covering her laughter. "Not funny, Di." He grunted. "What are you looking for?" She asked. Still rubbing his head, Terry responded. "My Dad gave me a bottle of Cognac when I got my first field assignment." Diane tilted her head in bewilderment. "Is that when we went to the Everglades?" Terry grunted confirmation. "Yep." Diane, who had been beside Terry, walked around to face him, irritation lining her face. "Was that during our honeymoon?" She asked, anger in her voice. Mocking her, Terry tilted his head. "Now that you mention it, Yes." He stated bluntly. Diane squinted at him. "Would you mind telling me why you didn't break out this expensive, smooth drink on our special night?" She urged with a bit of aggression. Terry smiled. "Not at all." He replied and went back to digging in the boxes for the Cognac. Diane took offense, thinking Terry was dismissing her. "Terry!" She whisper-shouted. (A way of shouting at Terry without disturbing the twin's nap. "What?" He whispered back. "You didn't answer my question. Terry paused, stood up smiling, holding a bottle of Cognac. "My love," He began. "I wanted to save this for a special night; our honeymoon was not special." Terry began. In that second, Diane thought her world exploded. "What?" she whispered in disbelief. Terry touched her cheek. "Not special, my love; it was miraculous. You are a miracle made real, and I did not want to soil our union by inebriating myself in a manner that would prevent me from enjoying our coupling. Tonight, tonight is special because I've begun a new chapter with the love of my life, blessed with children that are miracles themselves, and now I get to ponder the future of my family with my mate." Diane's eyes began streaming with tears. "You are such an asshole, Terry." Terry smiled, knowing exactly what she meant, which did not prevent her from verbalizing her thoughts. "You know you didn't have to put me through that emotional rollercoaster." She snapped at him while punching him. Terry cut his eyes at her. "Hey, turn that punch into something productive." Terry jokingly insisted. Diane smiled and jumped into his arms, giving him rapid kisses on the neck and face, which usually tickled Terry. Coaxing the desired results, Terry cringed and said. "Stop." Seeing her opportunity, Diane doubled down and began to growl as she kissed him. Terry broke down and began laughing. Diane approached him harder, and Terry laughed loudly, adding his pleas. "Baby, please. stop." He gasped. Diane relented. As they lay there getting their breath back, Diane whispered. "Shh." She hushed her husband. Terry strained to hear, following his wife's que; then he heard the twins laughing. Terry looked at Diane. "Good job." Diane smiled. "Put the bottle away for later." came her suggestion. Terry nodded. "Try not to hide it on yourself again." She teased. After flicking his wife the finger, Terry entered the twin's room. As he expected, Lance sat up while Ellie was on her back playing with her toes. When Terry entered, they both turned their heads to look at him. Their stare's intensity made Terry feel like he was in the crosshairs. Terry shrugged off the feeling and, without knowing it, began a tradition. "What's up?" He asked playfully. To his astonishment, the two began babbling at him. Nonsense, of course, but with structure, as if in their minds, they were speaking. "Diane," Terry called out to his wife. A moment later, Diane entered the room to find her husband sitting in the middle of the room, and much to her astonishment, the babies were both chattering at Terry. What threw her in a loop was how the twins, upon her entry, ceased talking to Terry and stared at her as if to gauge what she would do. When all Diann did was stand there, amazed at what she saw, the twins began babbling at her; Terry motioned for Diane to sit beside him. She slowly sat beside him, and the twins uttered structured nonsense for the next ten minutes. Diane was breathless. "Terry, they're trying to verbalize." Diane expressed shock. Terry nodded. Staring at his children and feeling ridiculous, Terry attempted to converse with a barely a-year-old child. "I understand you're trying to talk to us, and I don't know how much you understand, but it's going to take some time before we can understand you." Terry tried communicating. Terry thought he was beyond being surprised since Lance and Ellie were born, but they were showing how wrong that assumption was. When Terry expressed his disappointment at being unable to communicate with them, Lance sighed and reached out to Terry, who leaned toward his son and hugged him as if to console him. Terry accepted the hug and slowly pulled away, and Lance babbled. "S,awigh," Diane whispered. "Did he just say, "It's alright in baby talk?" Her voice dripped in awe. Terry nodded. "I think he did." Was his response of disbelief. "Maybe that elder medicine woman is on to something," Terry observed.

CHAPTER 10

New Home

The Elders gathered in the community hall as was requested by the tribal Chief. Terry and Diane entered, found a place to sit, and waited while the rest of the town gathered. The Elder, who introduced himself as John, took to the podium. "Kwe." He said in greeting. My brothers and sisters, I greet you in harmony and wish our new neighbors welcome. Turning to Terry and Diane, giving a short bow. "Anamikagage, welcome. We thank you for making yourselves available for our questioning." John espoused. Terry stood. "We should thank you for such a warm reception," Terry said gratefully. "Why are you here?" John asked candidly. Not taken aback by his forthrightness, Terry repaid it by being equally direct. "My wife and I are conservationists and meteorologists, Doctors of the Earth. Before our babies were given to us by the Great Mother, we worked in the south measuring everything from air quality to bacteria production." Terry explained. "For what purpose?" John inquired. Diane stood beside her husband and held his hand, a gesture that did not escape the elders. "My husband and I have noticed that the Mother of all is ill. Her skies, water, and Earth have conquered our greed and sickness." Diane complained. "The elders nodded. "We, too, have noticed. The Mother is sick, but not us made her so." John exclaimed. "We know that sir," Terry interjected. "We only see that she is. My wife and I have brought our children here to your land to help study the sickness and search for a cure." He exclaimed. "What kind of bullshit are you trying to sell?" A young man stood shouting and receiving a cheer from the younger members. Terry breathed deeply. "I understand your distrust, but I have never lied to you or broken any promises. What the government has done to you and all the tribes of this land, I also cannot speak on. I can only speak for myself and my family. I am Terry Rogers. Adopted son of Winston and Sheryl, husband to Diane Silver-Rogers, Father to Lance and Ellie. We are here because your people have more of a connection with the Mother than we ever had and hope to add your knowledge to ours to find a cure to what ails her." Terry concluded. John stood. "You spoke well, son of Winston. We of the black foot nation accept your offer of aid, for we, too, have noticed the Mother's ailment. We will do what is in our power; you will have our protection and cooperation. You will serve us in helping the Mother of all recuperate. I, John, spotted the owl of the Siksika, so claims." The noble leader promised. Terry bowed." Thank you, sir. Do you have any questions for us?" Diane inquired. An older woman stood up and shuffled over to Diane and the children. Diane stood with both babies; the older woman began to inspect Ellie and Lance. The woman sniffed the baby's feet, peered intensely into both eyes, and smelled their breath. She then mumbled in Lance's ear. His eyes widened, and to Terry and Diane's surprise, Lance laughed hysterically. Diane looked at Lance, deeply concerned. The Elder looked at Diane, smiled, and shook her head. For whatever reason, Diane understood that as a message: "Don't worry." Diane appeared to relax. The older woman then leaned close to Ellie's ear and whispered. Much to Diane's chagrin, Ellie's response was the opposite of her brothers. Where Lance laughed hysterically, Ellie wept. Her green eyes sparkled with tears; those tears turned into streams as they flowed down the pretty girl's face. Diane looked to the older woman, who (much to Diane and Terry's shock) found the Elder on her knees before Ellie and was followed by the rest of the council. Terry looked to John for clarification. Slowly rising, John looked at Terry and Diane, smiling. "We recognize the blessings our great Mother has graced our children with." John intoned solemnly. The implication did not escape Diane. "What do you mean by Our children?" Diane inquired, hoping her tone did not carry her anxiety. Looking at Diane sadly, John explained. "We see the great Warden of the Forest in the babies, and she that would speak for the great Mother. Do you now understand why I said our children?" John both explained and inquired. Diane stared at the elder Chief and slowly nodded. "Understand that no mother wishes to hear that her child is not her own and to predict with such certainty that one's children will soon no longer be theirs is…" Diane trailed off, close to tears. John spoke in tender tones. "It is not us who wish to separate you from the children, but we spoke a riddle to Lance, who found it amusing; to us, this spoke of the joy of life and its beauty. To Ellie, we spoke of wilting flowers and falling leaves, and her response spoke of the sadness Nature must endure as her colder aspects spoke of the silencing of her songs, which caused Ellie to cry, showing us she was in harmony with the Mother's vibrations." John proclaimed. Diane looked blankly at John. "I understand the words but not the meaning," Diane confessed. John bowed. "Your time and work with us shall clarify everything." John iterated. Terry extended his hand to the Chief; John clasped Terry's forearm. "You are family among us, and we thank you for blessing us with the care of these twins," John exclaimed. Terry grasped the forearm tightly. "We do not pretend to understand your ways, but if you would be patient with us," John raised his hand, interjecting. "Please, brother, You and your wife have much to do raising the children and your work; our ways will become familiar to you as you live among us; please do not concern yourself with our ways; they will soon become your ways." John consoled. Terry nodded. "We will follow your advice, John." Terry agreed. John smiled and turned to the assembly. "Brothers and sisters. Thank you for your time, patience, and understanding; we will gather again soon; go in peace." John said dismissively.

CHAPTER 11

Terra's State

Walking up to the shoreline, Terra listened to the waves as they gently broke upon the shore. The sun was at its zenith; wispy cirrus clouds streaked the blue backdrop that was the clear sky. A warm breeze gently tugged at Terra's robes. Calling to Gia's spirit that rested in the waters. *"Mother, Mother, hear my call."* She silently pled. A seagull flew close to Terra and began to squawk. Dozens of them soon followed it. The gulls called out in harmony, and the waters around Terra started to stir. The stir turned into a small whirlpool that seemed to gather water unto itself and form the figure of a Woman that rose from the center of the maelstrom.

"Mother." Terra exhaled as if exhausted. *"Daughter."* The water figure projected." Terra felt great relief at seeing her Mother again. *"Mother, why haven't you come to me? Didn't you see I need help?"* Terra projected heatedly. *"You never called the child."* The water figure projected. *"Really? I had to call out, although you can see I need help?"* Terra responded. Irritation becomes anger. *"Why are you so upset, child?"* The Gia essence projected. *"Why? I just told you why. The real why is, why have you never come to my aid?"* Terra wailed. *"Look around you; calm yourself."*

Gia directed. Terra looked and saw storm clouds gather, lashing out with streaks of lightning, a reflection of her anger. Terra paused, calming herself. The clouds soon parted, and the blue skies returned. *"Daughter, I have not come until now because I want you to have all the liberty you need. I wanted you to rest assured the seat of NatureNature is yours. You were always strong-willed and adventurous; I did not wish to hinder that. If you recall, my last words were that I rest in the waters, and you need me. All you had to do was call. As the millenniums passed, I saw you handle things very well. I see now that you are distressed."* Gia shared.

Terra nodded. "Mother, you don't know the mischief these children practice on each other; the joy they derive from evil intent and execution is appalling," Terra complained aloud. "It is part of the compromise," Gia responded. Terra sighed. The idea of Lucifer embedding fear as the dominant reactive emotion seemed brilliant initially. The seemingly simple act, while at first clever and placed the Nature of humanity quickly in Nature's grasp, has recently turned the helpful instinct into a world-destroying issue of control. As humanity became more sophisticated, so has its manipulation of all things natural and unnatural. The first Lie was that Mankind was superior to Nature. The second Lie was when humanity believed themselves to be more significant than the Source of Creation. Their hubris is exhibited by the way they treat their planet, their religion, each other, and even themselves. They consume what they know to be poisoned; They lay their waste with no thought of the effects on the environment. They go to war for profit and the theft of resources. Terra paced along the shore. "Mother, humanity has become insane." She whined softly. *"Daughter, my mandate was to bring into being a species that would one day evolve and begin their journey to Infinity."* Gia shared. Terra nodded. *"Yes, Mother, as you've explained, but my question is whether we've chosen the right species. What if we had gone through five big mass extinction events? Maybe we could have found a more suitable creature?"* Terra posed. *"No child."* The spirit denied. *"I was compelled by Eternity that humanity was the species to evolve,"* Gia confirmed. Terra's eyes widened. "Mother, could the forces have been mistaken?" Terra asked, speaking the unspeakable. The whirlpool twirled silently for a moment. *"Mother?"* Terra called aloud. *"Daughter, there is a great concern for your peace of mind. As humans become more powerful, they will become more destructive, causing you harm. The twin forces are mindful that in vindictiveness, you may surpass your authority and punish humanity in a manner they would never recover."* Gia warned. Terra listened gravely. *"What do you suggest, Mother?"* Terra probed. *"Something that may be beyond your abilities, my child,"* Gia warned. Terra looked at the shoreline. "All I can do is try, Mother." Terra espoused sensibly. *"True."* Nature agreed. *Daughter, you love all of your Creation but must find a way to love and let go without anger. Do not take the actions of humanity personally; remember, no mother hates their child because of their growth spurts."* Gia consoled. Terra cringed at the minimization of humanity's barbaric treatment of their home. The rampant pollution and their stubborn refusal to do anything meaningful regarding proper disposal. Images of massive amounts of garbage being dumped in Oceans. Landfills burning waste filled the sky with huge plumes of black smoke. Factories spew their toxins by the metric tons, contributing to the ever-worsening state of our air. Cities that once had pristine blue skies were now laden with a haze that forced people with weak respiratory systems to take appropriate measures for their safety. It was a matter of way too little and far too late. By the time humans admitted to their impact on the delicate ecosystem. "I don't think it will be as simple as forgive and forget, Mother," Terra complained. "I think you have been at rest for too long. While you slumbered, the peace of the Eternals was upon you, and as well deserved as that was, it also detaches you from your Creation, making you less concerned for the immediate because you're focused on the grand picture." Terra concluded. "That may be so child, but I am here now, not to supplant but to aid you." Gia posed. Terra looked up quickly and was surprised to see her Mother in all her glory and living flesh standing knee-deep in the water. Terra threw herself into her Mother's arms. "I've missed you, Mother," Terra whispered in her ear. Gia hugged her daughter tightly.

Walking miracles

The tribe elders loved the twins and showed affection through education, correction, and attention. Lance and Ellie kept their parents on their toes. From infancy to toddlers, they did as all children who feel loved and safe do; they were curious about everything. Diane may have had doubts about her children's exceptionalism before, but that quickly eroded as they continued to impress with simple yet sublime observations. One morning, John knocked on the door. Sitting on his bed waiting for his parents to attend to him, Lance heard the knock and squirmed out of bed. He stopped short when Ellie asked in their language. "Ner going?"

Lance smiled at his Sister. "Potted ow ah you." He babbled in response, prompting an "o ay." from his Sister, who seemed to have understood. Lance proceeded to wobble to the door. Reaching to grab the doorknob, Terry, dripping wet, with a towel tightly cinched at his waist, grabbed Lance's hand. "No, Lance, we don't do that." Terry admonished gently. Lance pursed his lips as if insulted. "Potted ow." He declared, pointing at the door. "What?" Terry asked, finding himself once again. The knock sounded again, causing Terry to jump slightly. "Potted ow!" Lance again demanded, pointing at the door. Terry opened the door and laughed. "Potted ow!" He exclaimed. John looked at Terry as if he were insane. Lance opened the door wider and called to John. "Potted ow." John had a huge smile on his face. "Yes, little one, I am John spotted owl." The Elder agreed. Terry realized his attire and pardoned himself. "John, my apologies; as you can probably see, I've had a hectic morning." Terry explained. "Yes," John agreed. "I can see that." Terry tilted his head. "Sarcasm?" He probed. "No, thank you. My wife made sure I didn't leave home without it." Terry Laughed. "Please, make yourself comfortable; grab a coffee if you'd like. I'm sure Lance can keep you entertained while I make myself presentable." John smirked. "Are you not presentable now?" Terry squinted, seeing where the conservation was going. "Not." Terry responded, being equally facetious. being recently confused by a child. The younger tribe members did as youth do, tease and challenge the twins. In great awe and some dismay, the twins eagerly accepted every challenge posed to them. Terry dashed up the stairs; Diane was drying herself as the couple shared a shower. "What was all the noise?" She inquired. "John was knocking, and Lance was about to open the door." He informed. "What?!! Diane responded, sounding worried. Terry explained the events that occurred. "Lance knew who it was before the door was opened. "Excuse me?" Diane questioned. Terry nodded. "That's right, except he called him "Potted Ow." Terry laughed. Diane wore a serious expression. While she knew what was occurring, Diane was not overjoyed seeing her children singled out. Terry eased her burden with a simple observation. "We always knew Lance and Ellie were not what most would call normal." Terry declared. "These are noble and trustworthy people, Diane; we should consider ourselves lucky that they took such a liking to them." He pointed out. Diane squinted at Terry. "I'm not stupid. I know we're lucky; you're forgetting I'm a mother, and that's what we do." Diane growled. Terry raised his hands in a gesture of submission. "No doubt, I just want…" Diane growled louder. "I know what you want, Terrence!" She snapped. Terry nodded and called out. "I'm thinking about going hiking; anyone wants to come?" He called out. Immediately, the twins, in unison, shouted from downstairs, shouted. "I do." Terry smiled at Diane, who scowled at him. Dressing in jeans and a tee shirt, Terry kissed Diane. "When you're ready, John is downstairs, and I think he wants to talk to the both of us." Terry remarked as he was about to exit the room. Diane, who had been slowly dressing, paused momentarily, displeased at the interruption. "You tell John," She paused, not wishing to allow her feeling to offend their host possibly. "Tell John I'll join you in a moment." She proffered. Terry, noticing her pause, smiled. "Will do, babe." Terry acknowledged the inner turmoil his wife just went through. *Nothing is more important to Diane than family. Perhaps because her folks are academics, she's trying to ensure Lance and Ellie get all the love she feels her parents didn't give her. Not that Niel and Esther didn't love their child, but an academic life is not always conducive to raising children."* Terry pondered. "John?" Terry called out when he reached the bottom of the steps. "We are here." John called from the den. Entering the spare room, Diane fashioned into a den; John spotted an owl between Lance and Ellie, who seemed to be tag-teaming The Tribal Chief by spewing childish gibberish with linguistic structure. "Children." Terry called softly. The two stopped babbling. "Pardon the children, John. The Elder of the clan sat, a look of awe plastered on his face. Diane descended the stairs to find silent children staring at their Father. A Tribal Chieftain was sitting with a stunned expression and tears on his face. Trying to maintain a sense of self-control, Diane asked. "What is going on?" As if a faucet was turned on full, Terry, John, Ellie, and Lance began to excitedly tell their perspective of the event that fostered their current predicament. "I came into the room, and," Began Terry. "Lance greeted me and was joined by Ellie, who began John. "Potted ow wanna know why…" Lance injected. "Me no wan potted ow be no understand everything." Diane paused a moment, then, as if a light was turned on, everything the children babbled in their broken language (which she took for twin talk.) It made sense to her, and she translated what they said to her husband and guest. Gesturing for quiet, Diane clarified for her children. "Chief, obviously, to the children, you are Potted Ow," Diane smiled. John returned the smile. Ellie claims Spotted Owl wants to know why. and Lance says He wants you to know everything." Diane interpreted. John appeared ten years younger. Diane rubbed her eyes, thinking she was hallucinating. "Are you alright, honey?" Terry probed. "Yeah, I'm fine." She evaded. "John, are you okay?" Diane asked the still-seated Elder. Slowly, John, spotted owl, Elder and Tribal chief of the Siksika clan of the Black Foot Nation, rose to his feet. Diane thought of the sun rising as she stared at a man with a purpose. Terry had a look of boyish glee on his face, and the children chanted in time, "man-it-ous-" man-it-ous "man-it-ous." John unexpectedly Shouted. "Surprising, Terry. Diane and John grinned at one another as if coming to an unspoken understanding. The twins smiled at John and bowed to the Elder, who returned it. "WE must allow the Alsoome to examine the children closely. I believe her initial gaze missed a great deal, and Lance and Ellie have a powerful message to spread if my suspicions are correct. They have powerful medicine, Diane," The Chief focused on her. "But nothing can be done without your blessing." The Chief uttered respectfully. Diane nodded. "I'm beginning to understand." She whispered. "I'm not sure that I do," Terry complained. John put his hand on Terry's shoulder. "All will be made clear, my brother," John reassured him. "I certainly hope so." Terry quipped.

CHAPTER 12
Consequences Unfold

New York City. The place everyone associates with Broadway plays, fine dining, outstanding parks, and its multi-cultures, the great melting pot. This morning, it was bright with the end of winter nip in the air. Benny Torres jumped out of bed and ran to the kitchen table to scarf down his breakfast. "What's the hurry, Papi?" Benny's Mother asked. Celeste and her husband Antonio came to the great city as most do. Immigrating from Nicaragua, they worked hard to provide little Benny with everything they never had. "Me and Carlos are going by the docks and doing some fishing," Benny replied. "Okay, but you be careful, mojo." Antonio admonished. Kissing his wife, Antonio rubbed his son's head and exited the apartment. Celeste looked at her son. "I made lunch for you and put it in the fridge. There are ten dollars on the dresser if you need anything. Are you going to be okay?" She inquired with concern in her voice. Benny smiled. "Mom, we do this same thing every day. Of course, I'm going to be okay. you and Pop raised me to care for myself, and I do." Benny bragged. "Yes, you do, mojo. You are so grown at seventeen." Celeste agreed with pride. "Okay, clean your plate, have fun, and be careful." She warned as she prepared to leave for work. Benny smiled. "Like I told Dad, me and Carlos are gonna do some fishing, maybe chill at the park," Benny informed his Mother. Celeste nodded her approval and hugged her son. "Be careful, baby." She urged while kissing him. As she exited the door, the phone rang. Celeste stopped at the door to see if the call was for her. She heard Benny laughing. "Who is that, Benny?" She impatiently asked. "It's Carlos's mom." He responded. "Yeah, man, you about ready?" Benny probed. "Yeah, I'll be at the docks in a half hour." Carlos agreed. "Cool, see you there," Benny confirmed. Benny hung up the phone, grabbed his backpack and fishing pole, and went to the fishing docks near Sheepshead Bay. After an amusing train ride (Train rides in New York were sometimes funny; sometimes, they were dangerous but rarely dull.) Exiting the train at Voorhies Avenue. Stop. Benny walked to a local convenience store and bought a soda before proceeding to the docks, where his friend Carlos waited. Dodging traffic, Benny crossed the busy avenue, enduring only one horn being honked at him, and another driver hurled some colorful expletives, which Benny repaid with a fully extended middle finger. Running up to his friend Carlos (who witnessed the exchange between Benny and the foul-mouthed driver, he asked in foul language, "What the fuck is his problem?" Carlos laughed. "Who knows, who cares? Let's fish." Benny exclaimed. "Fuckin right." Carlos agreed. The boys baited their fishing poles, and Benny turned to Carlos. Lunch to whoever hooks the biggest fish." He challenged. "Okay." Benny agreed. "Hope you brought real money 'cause you aint bringing me to no Mac D's or bogger king," Carlos complained. "You aint gotta worry about that 'cause yo punk ass couldn't even catch a cold." Retorted Benny." Carlos looked at his friend, pretending to be in pain. "That was so corny it hurt." He complained, holding his stomach. Benny smiled and complained. "Yo, that thing I gave that fool that honked at me, I now present to you." Benny then bowed to Carlos, shooting him the finger. Carlos laughed as both boys cast their lines into the water and did what fishermen have done through the ages; they waited. The wait was not long before Carlos's pole line went taut. "Aha!" Carlos grabbed the pole and began reeling it in. "Looks tiny. It didn't even bend the pole a little bit." Benny observed. "Listen, fool. The bet is not who's pole bends the most; if you don't catch no fish, you lose, fool." Carlos laughed. Carlos reeled in a decent-sized flounder. "Ohh, would you look at that? What do you get, Benny? Aww, you didn't catch anything?" Carlos teased. "Man, you can go…" Benny began but ceased as he jumped up to prevent his fishing pole from flying into the bay. "What the fuck?" Carlos wailed. Benny had snatched his pole from the air; now standing at the edge of the dock, Benny held a fully bent pole; struggling, he looked to his friend. "Hold on, Benny, don't let that bitch go." Carlos encouraged. The pole snapped in half in Benny's hand, sending him staggering back a few feet. A gathering of onlookers watched as the young man fought to land what most assumed was a record-breaking catch. Seeing the pole snap, they dissipated as a scream made them look toward the wail. To everyone's surprise, boats were being tipped over. First one, then a cascading effect as one after another was tipped over, and the bay was filled with people who were somehow dunked into the water. Then the carnage began. Screams filled the air as blood colored the seas. Carlos and Benny watched from the docks as screams of pain filled the air. In near shock, Benny tugged at Carlos. "C'mon, we gotta help." Carlos yanked his hand back. "Fuck that! I'm not going in that water." He argued. Benny shook his head and pointed to a lower part of the docks where they could pull people from the water. Carlos nodded in agreement and ran alongside his friend to help. The bizarre incident was reported on the news and was dismissed as a "Strange occurrence currently under investigation." They showed footage of two brave young men reaching from their position, pulling people out of the bay. The report also shared that there were over one hundred and fifty casualties. Later that night, as Antonio and Celeste watched the news, they were shocked to see their son on Television. Antonio stood abruptly. "Did Benny say anything about this to you?" He asked. Celeste shook her head in denial. Antonio turned and walked to his bedroom; Celeste followed, not knowing what her husband would do. Antonio opened the door, and Benny rolled over; covering his eyes, he called out. "Dad? Dad, what's going on?" Benny inquired nervously. "I just watched the news; guess who I saw?" Antonio asked rhetorically. "Dad, I didn't know what to do, all those people," Benny was surprised when his Father walked over and hugged him. "I am very proud of you, son," Antonio whispered. Benny hugged his Father in return. Celeste quietly shed some tears, grateful her son was alive.

State of irritation

Terra stood on a raised sand bar. The ocean offered gentle waves where she stood. In her anger, Terra began to reveal how they treated her to the humans. It was a twisted rendition of Dorian Gray, where the evil deeds of the protagonist never touch him but are reflected in a portrait of himself. Humanity dumps upon Nature, and she bears the brunt of the foulness that is their waste. However, Nature puts in a new twist of retribution. The Salween River in Brazil has become so toxic it is considered the most polluted on the planet. The fishing communities had shut down and started selling glass and plastic. A city was built beside the Tiete River. The town has grown into an industrialized city. The river became so severely polluted that it developed a thick, foul-smelling layer of toxic foam. The foam emits a harmful hydrogen sulfide gas. Terra could taste it. A foul, bitter taste that was sharp. Terra was trying to be compassionate, but it seemed as if for all the good she does for the world, humans might be fascinated by the beauty for a moment, but that is as long as that experience lasts as poor human beings seemed unable to relax. In her fury, she lashed out, sending an invading species of flesh-eating fish to a community in New York that terrified the citizenry. However, Nature also witnessed bravery. The type that allowed a being to put their lives aside for someone else. For Nature, that signified sacrifice, and She knew very well. It pleased Terra to witness such willingness to save another that after the initial attack where property damage was minimal and the lives taken? Far less than her original intention due to the courage of two young men. Her attention was immediately called upon as Nature's children of the Amazon forest could be heard. The complaints of the trees were the loudest as ancient trees called to her, demanding protection against the razes of life that tore through their majesty without regard to the seedlings, saplings, or the elders of the Forrest. With that call followed the wails of the animal life. Their complaint was the diminishing of food sources. As it was dwindling at an unsustainable rate. The threat of extinction was upon them. Last but not least were insects and marine life. With their quiet voices, the marine life complained about an inability to breathe in the waters as it became saturated with mines and lumber industry pollutants. The insects complained of massive displacements as humans tore through the ground, destroying the homes of insects that had adhered to their duty of aeration, introducing air to the soil, and improving drainage to prevent the Forest from becoming a swamp. The job has become nearly impossible due to human interference, and if this system collapsed, that would mean the extinction of the entire Forest. Terra focused on her Amazonian jungle to assist. She encouraged certain weeds to grow longer as well as stronger. She increased the lethality of the Strychnos and the Oleander plants and coaxed the Rafflesia Arnoldi to proliferate wherever humans settled in the Forrest. This plant smells like rotting flesh, and Terra assumed humans would not tolerate such odors. Terra increased the hunter's urge in the Amazonian predators. The jaguar, the Black caiman, the green anaconda, the giant otter, the harpy eagle, the bull shark, and the electric eel. They became highly agitated and immediately began seeking humans to kill. Terra paused. Reflecting on her decision, she sought further advice; she called upon her Mother. In her manner, Gia rose from the waters. "Mother," Terra said in greeting. "My child." Was Gia's response. "The reason I called is simple." Terra began. "I imagine then this will be a brief visit." Gia conjectured. "I'm afraid so. I need your advice." Gia was silent; Terra began. "Mother, I have obeyed all of your strictures and the mandates of The Eternal and the Infinite," Gia interjected. "I hear a but coming," Terra smiled. "However," She continued. Humanity has taken it to the point where ALL of the Kingdoms have sent complaints and even a few from the fourth Kingdom." Terra pro-ported. What might have been the first time Gia was shocked? "The humans have reached out to you?" Terra nodded. "They have on a few occasions, but what I speak of is two young men that were ready to sacrifice themselves in aid of others." The sound of the waters carried Gia's voice. "What do you seek, daughter?" Terra reflected a moment before responding. "Are the two young men the aid you promised?" Gia was adamant in her response. "No. What you witnessed was the bravery of those who care; the two who will aid you shall be undeniable as they will share in your power and will fight for you, Terra, for the concept of a clean, healthy, and vibrant world that is the cradle for the next form of higher consciousness." Gia instructed. Finishing her statement, Gia returned to her rest and the form of the original Mother became a part of the sea. The world's noise returned in total volume as

Terra remembered pre-civilization peace when the Dryopithecus roamed the Earth during the Miocene era. It was a time of cleanliness and harmony when pre-dawn Humanity was more ape-like and were vegetarians, murder not being a part of their society, and with that modern thought came back the noise of the now shattering Terra's moment of nostalgia. Hearing pleas of desperation, Terra teleported herself to Turkey, where an earthquake felt in Syria was causing massive damage. With dexterity and speed, she stitched the fault line with two plates assaulting one another, causing massive Chaos to the humans caught in the affected area. Terra teleported to China without pause, where the Yellow River flooded, killing over nine hundred thousand people. Terra grieved for the loss of both Human and animal life. New Zealand was flooding because of cyclone Gabriel, which brought flooding and significant damage, and although only eleven people were counted among the dead, more than five thousand six hundred were still unaccounted for. Terra knew that if she did not get help soon, her response would be a calamity for humans. The spirits of the Kingdoms begged an audience, and Terra complied. In the abode of Nature, the spirits of the Kingdoms came with one missing. Plant, Animal, Insect. The one missing is the spirit of Humanity. "It would appear that some have become too good to be the company to them?" spoke a giant redwood. "So it seems." Agreed, a whale. "Humans have no purpose other than destruction." Complained a carpenter ant." Terra gazed at her family. "My children." She began.

CHAPTER 13

A Vision

Lance sat cross-legged, staring at his Sister, who had been in a deep state of meditation for most of the afternoon. She had suggested that perhaps it was time to try to reach out as the Alsoome had suggested. "Child," The Medicine woman advised. "You must call out to the Mother's spirit if you and the Warden hope to discover your purpose. It is for her that you have been gifted." She prompted. Lance felt a wave of despair; he looked at his Sister and noticed a tear slide down her cheek. Unwilling to disturb her, Lance impatiently waited. The trees waved with the breeze, and Lance could hear a faint moaning sound. *"Be still, brothers."* Lance projected; the moaning ceased. *"Where-for has gone the conduit?"* A mighty Pine inquired. Lance directed his stare at a majestic Pine Tree. "Brother, Nature's child seeks the Mother now," Lance responded, wishing his Sister would snap out of her trance. The sky was clear, and the mountain air was crisp though summer was upon them. Ellie sobbed aloud, bringing Lance from his self-reflections. "El?" Lance implored. "What's wrong, sis?" Ellie looked at her brother with sadness in her eyes. "I have found The Mother Lance," Ellie reported. "Great!" Lance responded. "Let's go tell her of the events; maybe she will repair what needs fixing."

Lance expounded anxiously. Ellie shook her head slowly. "What?" Lance prodded. Ellie gave a deep sigh. "Approaching the Mother now would be extremely dangerous." Ellie advised. "What?" Lance exclaimed, alarmed by Ellie's description. "The Mother is no longer rational. She has taken to viewing humanity as a threat. I believe she means to exterminate us." Ellie shared. "No fucking way!" Lance insisted. "Way." Ellie contended. "Well, there has to be something we can do to convince her otherwise." Lance insisted. Ellie pondered Lance's statement. "I have a difficult time changing your mind once you believe something, brother; I can't imagine the stubbornness innate in a being as powerful as Nature herself." Ellie observed. Lance nodded. "That makes terrifying sense." Lance agreed with his sisters' assessment. "Why were you crying, sis?" Lance asked, making her aware that he had witnessed her earlier display of sadness. Ellie shook her head. "I felt her sadness, Lance. The Mother is distraught over the ambivalence of humanity. She loves us yet is repulsed by us, and the contradiction does not sit well with her." Ellie shared, staring into the bright blue sky. Lance stared at the sky. "Perhaps if I started in the Amazon jungles?" Lance probed. "Started what?" Ellie inquired. "The war." Lance responded. "What?!!" Ellie responded; disbelief was heard in her exclamation. Lance stared at his Sister. "I think I should go into the Amazon forest and give them an ultimatum." Lance asserted. "What will you say that will make them change their minds? You are aware that greed drives them," Ellie insisted. "Well, Lance began. First, I'd ask them to stop, then explain the harm caused by removing the trees." Lance continued. "I would also explain why money would not be an issue without a planet." Lance concluded. Ellie looked severely at Lance. "And you think an environmental speech will curtail the decades-long practice of the lumber industry? Is that what you think, Lance?" Ellie giggled. "Why are you laughing at me, El?" Lance asked, sounding irritated at Ellie's laughter. "Oh, my beautiful nieve brother. They will only laugh at you and tell you nothing is more valuable than profit. Lance became angry. "Then I will offer the ultimate authority! it will be war!" Lance insisted. Ellie laughed harder. "War?" Ellie asked. "Against whom? with what are you going to fight?" Ellie inquired, curiosity peeked. Lance appeared to have grown a foot or so. "Against humanity, and I will fight with my army." He insisted. "What army?" Ellie asked. The shade that protected them from the sun. Darkness descended rapidly, yet Ellie knew the sun had not set. Ellie looked up and saw layers of trees lining up beside Lance. "My army." He revealed with open arms. "I shall go to the Amazon and present my offer there." He stated. "And if they refuse?" Ellie postured. Lance smiled. "Then my brothers of the Amazon shall rise in defiance, and the mortals will learn." Lance spat. "I do not agree with this course of action, Lance." Ellie argued. Lance nodded. "I understand, Sister, but what would you have us do? Remember, although Nature loves her creations, she recognizes the need to kill off portions of them to make the grand plan of the Eternals come to fruition." Lance pointed out. "Please, sis, don't stand in my way." Lance pled. Ellie sighed, knowing she couldn't refuse her twin. Clouds of transparency and lift gathered around the feet of Lance, who looked up at his Sister and smiled. "Thanks, sis." Lance voiced his appreciation. "Just don't get yourself killed." Ellie complained as Lance was lifted into the air and then concealed as he was propelled to the Amazon rainforest. Ellie stared at the space where she had last watched Lance disappear over the horizon. Ellie focused on the sight, and before she was aware of it, she looked at her brother, using water droplets as her eyes; Ellie watched over her brother's flight. Wrapped securely yet gently, Lance flew over the Atlantic and was in awe of his sisters' powers. *"Remember what I told you."* Lance heard his Sister's voice as if it surrounded him. "El?" Lance called out loud. *"Yes, brother, I can hear you, but you don't have to speak; send your thoughts to the clouds."* She directed. "El, this is freaking incredible! The clouds act like a speaker system or something?" Lance inquired aloud. *"I don't know how it works, Lance, only that it does, and why are you speaking out loud? I'm trying to establish a silent communication with you, and you're just babbling."* Ellie complained. *"Okay, I get it."* Lance projected bitterly.

Insanities door.

Terra fought between her anger and sorrow. She was confused. *"Why does humanity hate me so much?"* She pondered. I will not go back to my Mother or the Eternals again. I must find a way to. Terra stopped as she heard a call. A call filled with sorrow and pain. Terra had been hearing mounting cries of suffering and desperation for decades. This was only different because this voice was human and calling out to her. Terra sought out the voice and found a young woman sitting beneath the shade of a tree where there were no trees. Terra listened to this supplicant's plea. *"Mother, I have searched for you. I know you are in pain; I know the source of the pain. I beg you to allow us to assist you."* The woman begged. "How is it that I can communicate with this woman?" Terra wondered. *"How could one such as yourself aid me?"* Terra challenged. Terra did not hear an immediate reply and thought the Human, like most, made nothing but another gesture. When suddenly, she heard a response. *"My brother, even now, is on his way to the jungles of the Amazon to convince the lumber and mining companies to cease the stripping of the forest and plundering of her resources."* The supplicant responded. Terra was unmoved. *"Many have gone with such notions only to come away empty-handed or with heavy pockets." Was Terra's response.* The supplicants' voices returned with the strength of conviction. "My brother does not accept no for an answer." Came the cold retort. Terra was impressed by the force of the reply and pushed the issue. *"And why would you fight for me against your own, and who are you that you would claim such authority?"* Terra queried. "Alsoome, my tribe's Medicine woman, has decreed me to be the embodiment of Nokomis, the earth guardian, and my brother has been dubbed Nikoskoa, Warden of forests, by the black foot tribe. My Mother named me Elinor, which means sunshine in our language. To answer more directly, I would fight anyone who attempts to destroy my home, and you, Mother, are our home." Was the reply. Terra considered Ellie's words. "You realize I've heard this promise before by your kind." Terra pointed out. Ellie sighed in resigned agreement. "Yes, Mother, I know that to be true. I can say that I never made such promises to you, but I swear. I will fight to defend you, even if it means killing off our species." Terra was taken aback as throughout her entire existence, she had never spoken with her charge directly, and yet this unknown entity who called herself Elinor swears undying support for all things natural. For the first time in a millennium, Terra did not feel alone. Her attention was distracted by a sizable hurricane starting in the Bahamas. *"I must go now, child; I will watch how and when you support me."* Terra promised before setting to rectify the rogue storm. "Look to the jungles of the

Amazon. You will find my brother with his army presenting their case." Ellie called out to the departing spirit. Terra was aghast at the thought of more military in her precious Forest. Catching the thought, Ellie projected. "It is not what you think, Mother. See how your son proudly battles for you." Ellie invited. Terra responded. *"Be sure that I will."* She promised. Overjoyed at the contact, Ellie reached out to her brother. *"Lance."* She projected. After a few seconds came Lance's response. *"What's up, El."* Ellie considered how much she should tell her brother. She told him about the entire visit of Nature from the initial approach to the information that Lance was in the Amazon about to go to battle for her." She iterated. *I wish you would have held off on the battle talk for a bit."* Lance confided. *"What's wrong?" She inquired. "Nature can be ruthless, El, and I'm trying to free these trees from the threat of impending death. I don't want to march these trees into certain death, and I'm afraid if the Mother is here, she'll send them all into the flames to garner a victory. I want to spare as many of these beautiful beings as possible."* Lance concluded. Ellie loved her brother's sense of fairness and compassion. "If anyone can do it, it's you, Lance." She praised her brother. "Thanks, El, I'll keep you posted." He terminated the link. Ellie began the trek back down the Mountain when a goat calmly walked beside her and gently butted her. Ellie stopped and looked down at the beast. Smiling, she reached into her bag and gave the Goat some nuts. Bleating with joy, the Goat ate greedily. Ellie began walking again when, to her surprise, the Goat gently bumped her. Ellie looked down and, feeling somewhat ridiculous, impulsively said. "My friend, I'm sorry, but I have no more food to share with you." Ellie looked around in the unlikely event that someone else was atop the Mountain. Seeing no one, she was surprised to look down at the Goat staring at her. Ellie tilted her head in curiosity. The Goat began bleating again; the difference this time was it had the cadence of speech. As Ellie listened, the bleating didn't become words, but they did become understandable. "Misstress, I am called Lip dancer by my herd. I will assist you decent if you would, but climb on my back. The Goat bleated. Ellie's smile was huge. "Lip Dancer, you say?" Ellie inquired. "Yes, Misstress. None are as sure-footed nor swifter than yours truly. It is why my tribe requested I escort you down the Mountain, great lady," The Goat bleated. Ellie blushed at the title. "I am no great Lady; may I call you a dancer?" Ellie probed. "Of course, my lady, but why would you deny who and what you are?" Dancer bleated. "I am the daughter of Terry Rogers and Diane Silver, and I am nothing special." She claimed modestly. Ellie climbed aboard the back of Dancer, who began a slow, comfortable pace. "That is not what the wind says, the ground we walk on, or the fact that you are conversing with a goat." Dancer bleated. Ellie laughed; curious, she asked. "What does the wind say, mighty Dancer?" Ellie poked. "The wind says you are imparted with the gifts of Nokomis, the earth spirit, and your brother is Nikoskoa, the Warden." The goat side pridefully." Hearing his tone, Ellie laughed. "And why do you sound so pleased?" She queried. "Because, my lady, I shall be royalty amongst my herd because I got to escort you to your home and speak to you; what message may I bring to my herd?" Dancer requested. Ellie thought a moment. "Tell them that the Warden and the Nokomis fight for the Mother, and we will establish balance again." She exclaimed. Dancer stopped. "Thank you, my lady." He bleated. Ellie realized she was coming out of the woods and heading toward her house. The streets began to fill with young and teenage tribesmen and women who started to cheer as Dancer led Ellie home. The front door to her home opened, and Terry and Diane stepped out as Ellie dismounted and kissed Dancer on his forehead. "Thank you, noble Dancer." She said softly. "My pleasure, my lady." Then, the Dancer performed an act never seen by a wild animal; the Dancer bowed. Tipping his chin to the ground and straightening, he bleated, turned, and walked back to a cheering audience. Terry and Diane hugged their daughter and led her into the house.

CHAPTER 14
Black Foot Reservation

Ellie and Lance trudged up the Mountain the tribe designated Ninaistako, meaning Chief Mountain. An oral tradition of the Mountain states, "Near the end of days, a great white god would appear from the top of the Mountain, and upon his departure, the Mountain would crumble. Climbing over a lip, Lance spied goats frolicking about. His Sister came up behind him. "It's beautiful up here," Lance observed. "Yeah, and I'm tired of always seeing things last," Ellie whined, coming up behind her brother. Lance looked at his twin with a look of reprimand. "El. You know why I always lead." Lance quipped. Ellie folded her arms. "No, Lance, I don't know that; why don't you explain that to me." She demanded. Lance stopped his walking and turned to his Sister. "Do you acknowledge that I'm stronger than you are?" Lance inquired. Ellie scowled. "So what? Is this some macho bullshit you and Dad spoke about?" Ellie inquired angrily. "El," Lance said calmly. "Have you forgotten what our medicine woman told our family on our sixteenth birthday?" Lance probed. Ellie flashed back a month before their sixteenth birthday observance, recalling how the Medicine woman, accompanied by Chief John, came to their home and sat with her parents before calling in the twins. "You have grown much, Nikoskoa," John observed of Lance as he entered. Lance bowed at the honorific. "Noble Chief, my growth is possible only by the grace of my parents and my Nation." Lance acknowledged. John smiled. "Well said, young warden." He complimented. Ellie entered the room, and the Chief and the medicine woman nodded to her. "What's all this?" Ellie inquired. "This, our daughter, is our medicine woman confirming you on your journey into womanhood, whether or not you are what we always expected you to be," John commented mysteriously. Ellie looked at her Father. "Dad, do you know what he's talking about?" She asked as if ignorant of what they spoke. Lance elbowed his Sister in the ribs. "Ouch." She complained at the jab. "Stop playing around," Lance demanded. "You're always so serious." She quipped. Ellie looked into the eyes of the Medicine woman. "Alright, grandmother, What say you?" She inquired. The Medicine woman lowered her head and began to chant. Ellie, who had been standing, plopped to the floor as she felt her strength leave her. She heard the chant continue, and then the strangest sensation overwhelmed Ellie, and she saw two stunningly beautiful women in the distance. She watched in awe as the women raised the grass, the trees, the animals, and even up to Mankind itself. The images changed to one woman who stood alone, and she had changed dramatically. The once beautiful woman looked sickly. Her once beautiful hair now looked stringy, her eyes hollow. Snapping out of the imagery, Ellie had tears in her eyes, and the medicine woman was on her knees, followed by John. "You are Nikoskoa, friend and Warden of the land," She expressed to Lance and you," She looked at Ellie. "You have revealed yourself to be Nokomis; the spirit of the Earth goddess is with you." She explained.

"Ellie. El!" Lance shouted, snapping her out of her reverie. "So what? Are you supposed to be my protector or something?" She asked, sounding upset. Lance grinned. "Of you and the land," said Alsoome, our medicine woman." Lance agreed. Ellie followed her brother silently. Lance noticed the air became very till, and a silence fell over the Mountain. Ellie stopped in her tracks. Seeing his Sister Lance also froze, he began to listen. The strangest thing occurred. It was as if Lance was connected to all the trees, and their leaves became his eyes. Dizzy from the massive information input, Lance sat heavily on the ground. A few feet behind her brother, Ellie rushed to him, seeing him collapse. "Lance, Lance,"

Ellie shouted. "C'mon, protector! Wake up. You got a job to do, so get up!" Ellie shouted at her brother. Lance stirred, looking at his Sister; he begged. "El, please stop shouting. I never knew you were so damned loud." Lance complained. Ellie hugged her brother. After a moment, she pulled away and asked. "What the hell was that?" Lance snickered. "From loving and caring to terrorizing in nothing flat, I give you she who would be the healer." Lance joked. Ellie shoved him. "That is so not funny," Ellie complained. "I want to know what happened to you?" Ellie demanded. Lance paused a moment while he collected his thoughts. "Well," He began. "It felt like I was pulled out of my body, then, all of a sudden, it felt as if I had a million eyes, which made me very dizzy, but it was like every tree became my eyes." Lance concluded in awe." Ellie was silent for a moment. "What did you see?" She asked after a moment. Lance nearly whispered. "Some alarming things, El. I think the great other of all is descending into madness." Ellie's mouth dropped open. "That can't be right." Ellie gasped. "Can it?" She asked, mystified. Lance told her what the tree's vision shared about the woman in Spain being torn apart. Another was consumed alive by bugs, and another bound by vines, held in place until the ground opened and swallowed him. Ellie shook her head in disbelief. "That can't be true," Ellie argued. Lance got to his feet again. "It is Sister, and I think you can find out exactly what is happening if you only open yourself to your gift. Ellie crossed her arms over her chest. "I can't believe…" Lance interjected. "Can't or won't?" Ellie looked off into the distance. "Can't, won't, what's the difference?" Ellie argued. Lance exhaled loudly. "El, you always want to assume the best; I say, why assume when all you have to do is what Alsoome told you to do, and you would have all the answers you need. Why do you think our Elders bowed to us, huh?." Lance pointed out. Ellie nodded and sat down.

Terra's Cave

Terra was overjoyed to see her Mother again. She explained to Great Gia all that had transpired since her departure into the waters. "Mother, have you not seen the devastation humanity has indulged in? This unruly race has attacked the sky, Earth, and waters!" Terra complained vehemently. "How can we have a mandate to protect and nourish a populace hell-bent on self-destruction?" Terra queried. For the first time in a millennium, Gia spoke. "My daughter, it is not in our mandate or prerogative to know the plans designed for humanity. Our mandate is to protect their existence. It is for the Infinite and Eternals to judge how they will achieve the grand plan meant for them." Gia shared with Terra. Unsatisfied with the response, Terra debated with her Mother. "How is it remotely possible that such savagery is rewarded?" An exasperated Terra demanded.

"Daughter, our powers of Creation were given to us by the ultimate Creators. We have no claim on Creation, and we do as was bid for us to do." Gia explained; however, she could see in Terra's facial expression that she was not getting through to her. "Daughter, I will depart with one piece of advice for you." Gia prefaced. "Try to realize that you are not alone. I've watched you handle this immense responsibility by yourself. You've only once come to me. You never call upon the Creators for aid or advice, and finally, had you been paying closer attention, you would have noticed the Creators have sent you a set of twins modeled after them to aid you. One is a Warden of the forests, and the other has the spirit of us born in her." Gia shared. Terra looked at her Mother in shock and awe. "Why didn't I know this? sense it?" A confounded Terra wondered aloud. "You have been far too busy. First, by trying to control humanity's mistakes, then by taking revenge against the insults hurled at you." Gia observed. Terra tried to control her rage, which the weather showed she was failing at as massive storm clouds gathered. "Unless you plan to sink many islands, I suggest you calm yourself," Gia suggested. Seeing the gathering clouds, Terra calmed herself. "What should I do then, Mother? With the constant pollution, weather tampering, toxic dumping of medical waste, and other chemicals, I'm not sure how much more I can take!" A desperate Terra pled. "Call to the Creators, my child. They have been and always will be there for you. Now I must depart back into the sea, for I was granted this form that I surrendered so long ago so that I may advise you if you need me; all you have to do," Terra interjected. "Is call you?" Gia smiled. "Yes, daughter," Gia replied as she returned to the sea, becoming one with it again. Terra stared at the spot where her Mother was. Only now did she realize how much she missed her Mother. Following her advice, Terra emptied her mind and cast it into the void. *"Welcome home, child."* A soothing yet very full voice said in greeting. *"What do you require of us?"* The irresistible and unmoving voice of Creation asked. *"My Lords, what would you have me do with the creation dubbed Humanity?"* Terra prompted. *"You wish to know if they still have our grace."* Was the response. Terra realized it was more of a statement than a question. *"I do, Lord." You may act to defend the Earth, but only in measures that will educate. Unless for edification, any threat to the existence of humanity will not be permitted."* The voice of Creation rang. Terra closed her mind to the void and returned to the present. She reflected for a moment on what was said and, for the first time, smiled.

In the Atlantic Ocean, a cargo ship to a European port carried freight from Japan of high-tech computer chips. The last message from the R.M.S. Neeland was that it ran into unexpected rough seas. The S.O.S. reporting a rogue wave was never received as the ship was swallowed whole, becoming part of the vast watery graveyard of the Atlantic. In Africa, it was reported that the Sahara received over a foot of rain, causing flooding in the driest region on Earth. In the Middle East, in Western Iraq, a monster sandstorm swept through most of the area. It was so large that the static build-up from the sand interfered with communication equipment. Hundreds of deaths were reported from accidents and electrical fires in textile plants. In Latin America, heavy rains and strong winds have isolated villages from flooding and mudslides. Terra focused on America, where airplanes were spraying chemicals in the air. Terra willed the air masses to swell until down draft versus updraft caused one plane to crash and others to be grounded until the weather cleared.

Terra returned her mind to the cave her body dwelled in. As her mind inhabited her body again, she felt compelled to look in a still pond and was shocked at the reflection. Her hair looked thinner, her face even more hollow; even though she felt better for the reprimand she had just inflicted on humanity, she speculated that her well-being was tied to the Earth and Mankind. The thought was both terrifying and infuriating. Why would the Creators bind the fate of a life-affirming entity to a barbaric, self-loathing species? Terra found herself more confused than ever as she began to ponder the motives of Creation. "How many have to die before humanity reaches the state of evolution before the Creative forces are satisfied? Then what? Do Billions? Do even Trillions die before such a state of enlightenment is achieved? Terra began to have very dark thoughts about the motives of the Creative forces, which in turn darkened her spirit, giving a chance for the spirit of Chaos to beguile her with promises of retribution and revenge for all the life lost under her care. *"Think of it, Mother, no longer will you be subject to the illusory whims of humanity. They are savages that shit where it eats and piss where it drinks while fornicating in the filth of itself."* The voice of Chaos crooned in the angry Mother's ear. Terra considered the voice; storm clouds gathered. *"Yes, Mother. Teach the upstarts that they may not violate the Mother's prerogatives without consequence. That Nature's law, not man's, is the only way to salvation, and by the grace of the Elders, they never specified how many had to make it to the next stage of evolution."* Chaos suggested. Terra smiled diabolically as if seeing a loophole that pleased her. "Yes, The Eternals never did specify how many of these loathsome creatures had to arrive at evolution's doorstep, did they?" She asked the now silent voice of Chaos. Terra paused a moment, recalling what her Mother had shared. Twins. Her Mother had said that the Eternals had sent twins to aid her, but Terra did not understand how two mortals could help even if modeled after The Creators. Curiosity stirred. Terra focused her mind on finding the twins her Mother spoke about. Even though Terra was not told the location, she felt confident she could see them; after all, not many walked with the aura of power these two must be emitting.

CHAPTER 15
Battle for the Amazon

Lance was gently put down in a densely packed portion of the forest. Getting his bearings, the first thing he did was establish communication with all the natural inhabitants of the forest to make his presence, identity, and mission known. Lance projected. *"Brothers, Sisters of all species, I call upon the largest and the smallest. Uncaring humans are ravaging your homes and lives. The Great Mother has heard your cries. I am here to present an ultimatum to the humans: cease any further destruction of my forest or face my wrath."* "Many voices, large and small, rang out almost immediately. Emotions ranged from anger to sorrow to fear. Lance remained calm although lambasted for inaction and indifference. Lance breathed to cleanse himself. "If you would allow?" He begged. The quiet forest grew silent, so much so that the different headquarters of the corporations stationed there grew very concerned over the silence that descended on a jungle that never slept. "My family, I have been dubbed "Nikoskoa, Warden of the forest. Entitled by my tribe members of the Blackfoot Nation and sanctified by the Mother. I have come to end this tyranny." Lance exclaimed. A huge pine that stood amongst a grove of them spoke through hissing leaves. *"Many have come with our dead cousins in their hands, making demands, but they were silenced.* Lance grunted. "I am not so easily silenced," Lance promised. "So you are prepared to go to war?" A tiny voice squeaked. Lance looked down at a small field mouse. "I am brave, brother; however, before I would subject you to more death than you've already suffered, I would speak with their leaders and give them a chance." Lance pointed out. "*This has been tried before. I've witnessed them kill their kind and dispatch their bodies in the jungle, never to be found.*" An owl hooted. Lance nodded. "That is the way of my kind." Lance concurred. "However," He continued. "We will not give them the war they are used to, no. We will use all that is at our disposal; we will use stealth, camouflage, and the forest herself to aid us." Lance exclaimed. All the headquarters of the region that wondered over the silence that blanketed the forest for over a half hour was suddenly shattered as everything alive lifted its voice in a shout of defiance.

The following morning, some corporate supervisors were listening to the complaints of different section chiefs, explaining how some of their equipment had gotten damaged in the middle of the night. Miners also found themselves in a predicament as cave-ins began around 2 am, and the cause was yet to be seen. Lance engaged in tactical guerrilla warfare, systematically attacking poorly guarded areas, inflicting maximum damage, and retreating before any response could be taken. During one such raid, Lance had all the termites ravage whatever wood support structures they could get their hungry jaws on. This action led to the closure of a copper and zinc mine. Lance focused on the lumber companies. It sent a message to the Arbor community to remain alert as the lumber companies seemed to resist any change to the current norm. Lance also recruited the Black Caiman and poison dart frogs to line the river banks, Bull sharks, and Piranha to guard the waterways with dolphins as interceptors. They would accomplish that by dragging sargassum, a type of seaweed, into their propellers, stranding boats to the currents of the mighty river.

Lance deployed vampire bats in the sky, and his ground troops consisted of trees from the Palm to Rubber, Kopok, Ramon, Xate, and the majestic Angelim families. He was aided by the fast and deadly Jaguer, the agile Spider monkey, the furious-looking Bald Yukari, and the wild and powerful Howler. His secret weapon was the insects of the Amazon.

The morning mists found security guards facing a lone man outside the Kogo Lumber Inc. gates. "You are trespassing. You will be arrested if you don't leave the area immediately," the guard warned. Lance tilted his head. "It is you that trespass. Who invited you here? Who permitted you to raze our forests? Destroy our wildlife, pollute our," "Listen, buddy," the guard interrupted.

"We are here legally. We have contracts with your government to be about our business, so unless you want to get arrested, I suggest you go about yours." The guard threatened. "I see," Lance responded. "See, don't see. Frankly, I don't give a shit. So why don't you call your picketing buddies so they can take you home before you get hurt." The guard growled, attempting to intimidate Lance. "So you don't want to report this to your superiors so we may reach an amenable conclusion?" Lance inquired. The guard laughed. "Are you serious or stupid?" He asked. Lance tilted his head, smiling. "So that's a no to my request?" The guard took out his nightstick and picked up his walkie-talkie. "Yeah, we have an intruder that refuses to leave; send some back up to the main gate." The guard requested. Lance's smile deepened. "You are either very foolish or incredibly stupid." He observed. The guard laughed as jeeps full of armed security men arrived. "You know what, boy? You got a big mouth, and you stupid as shit thinking you could come into the forest alone and start some movement?" Lance looked around at the gathered men. "Gentlemen, I afford you this one opportunity to leave; you have come uninvited; you rape and pillage my forest with no thoughts of conservation. You are now evicted from these lands, never to return." Lance bellowed with a powerful voice that was carried by the winds. Taken aback by the power of Lance's say, the stubborn, well-paid guard reacted. Hurling himself at Lance and swinging his club, he hit nothing. Where Lance had stood was only air. A voice rang and echoed in the forest. "So be it."

"Invaders! Destroyers of the Mother's beauty. You come uninvited, unwelcome, and unwanted. We've asked, we pled. Your response is ridicule and violence. In the name of the Mother of us all, we give you this final opportunity to make amends. These are our terms. The money and time you took in destroying this place, put back into repairing the damage you've done, then go in peace." Lance proclaimed at the entry of one of many corporate giants. Standing on a main thoroughfare in front of a lumber company, He made his demands. "For far too long, you have benefitted from destroying innocent beings." Lance continued. A truck sped to the gates with uniformed guards. They were pulling up to the front entrance where Lance stood. The truck spewed para-military personnel. An officer exited the front of the truck and approached Lance, shouting. "You are on private property, and if you do not vacate the premises immediately, you will put me in a position of having to remove you forcibly." The officer warned. The jungle was quiet except for the truck's running motors. Lance's laughter broke the quiet. "The two-faced hypocritical gall of you saying this is private property and I'm not. We ARE NOT INVITED?!!" Lance thundered in a voice that carried well over the horizon. "Has arrogance turned your brain into mud? Or are you that genuinely stupid? You, sir, are uninvited. You, sir, are the usurper of the peoples and the will of the Forrest, and you shall suffer the wrath of the Warden. The officer signaled mercenaries jumped out of the vehicles, lifted their rifles, and pointed them at Lance. Suddenly, the sky grew dark, and the para-soldiers looked up. To their horror, they saw thousands upon thousands of bats descend upon them—hungry vampire bats whose hunger was maxed out. The creatures who had starved themselves for days at Lance's request promised them a feast beyond their comprehension. Lance delivered on his promise, and the bats would get their fill. Soldiers fired recklessly and, in their attempts to shoot the bats, only wound up shooting each other. Alarms began to ring, and many soldiers jumped into their vehicles as their livelihood was threatened. Lance released the Jaguars as a shock unit. Hitting swiftly, the big cats tore through the ranks of Corporate security, tearing at limbs and throats before disappearing into the forest. Soon, helicopters and boats could be heard coming in to reinforce the Corporate machine. Soldiers landed and deployed. Lance ordered his army to hide and wait. The difficulty for the corporate entities was that they had no idea of the strength of the opposing force. Seeing the enemy ease in their offense, The Milly Lumber company decided to fight back viciously. That evening, they deployed soldiers with flame-throwers, their orders? Burn all the brush within a one-mile radius of any primary corporate headquarters.

Lance heard the screams of underbrush burning. Roots cried for their offspring. Lance felt the deep sorrow of the trees and, in a fury, rose. "Brothers! Rise. Slay those who bring destruction to your doorstep. In a fury rise! In vengeance, rise, in the name of the countless deaths we've suffered, rise and visit upon them that they have brought you as a gift!" Lance Motivated his natural army. He called upon the meanest of his reserves, and the kingdom of the insect's world rose in blind fury, attacking the headquarters of the Lumber and mining corporations, killing thousands of workers. The insets of the Amazon are among the most poisonous. Many corporate supervisors fell to dart frogs as they ran for their boats. Some died from a vast number of bites from bullet ants, whose edges are excruciating. Corpses lay strewn across the jungle floor with insects invading their orifices—corporate sent reserves when reports were received by corporate regarding the fatalities. Mercenaries were sent up the river. The second phase of the attack was implemented as the boat props got tangled in thick weeds that Lance had called up just beneath the surface. The stalled boats were then attacked by huge four hundred pound Arapaima who rammed the boats, knocking the unsuspecting mercenaries into the river where they were dispatched by a combined attack of Piranha, Bull sharks, and Electric eels which ravage the men, causing the mighty Amazon river to flow red. The foot soldiers tried fighting off the Amazonian army to no avail. Impacted by a significant disruption to their facilities, corporate heads considered the massive financial loss in Amazon as the cost of doing business. This notion was unacceptable to the Developed Countries. A meeting was being called for by the most influential corporations in the world to discuss plans to resolve what they called a global crisis.

The crisis was not global but financial. The Amazon jungle was a tremendous source of natural resources that developed nations were not ready to release. The military campaign defeated the corporations and shifted the battleground, thinking the action was local. They refused to view it as a global event. The new battlefields would be the courts, or so they thought. In the United States, the situation was getting progressively worse as Canadian wildfires and wildly shifting weather patterns were wreaking havoc on the air quality and the environment in general. Florida was being slammed by a series of class three better hurricanes, doing massive damage to the shorelines and the infrastructure, with the cost running into the billions.

Meanwhile, the fires burned on the west coast, accompanied by mudslides. Earthquakes were on the increase. Confused and frightened, the populace responded to the uncertainty destructively and violently. Street crimes throughout the Country were increasing exponentially. Few connected the public's actions with what was happening in the world of Nature. Always believing themselves above Nature, no connection was made that the maltreatment of Earth was, in fact, an act of self-loathing and sabotage. Except for Ellie and Lance, who saw the wars, pollution, violence, and illness as all coming from the exact cause. Humankind's inability to be a part of his environment.

Lance reached out to his sister. *"El. El, we have to find the Mother."* Lance projected. A wind began to gather. The Forrest animals slowly approached him. "Brother and sisters. I am deeply sorry for the sacrifice you had to make today. You have your Forrest back, at least for a while. My Sister and I will take this battle to its next stage: to convince the humans if they wish to come here again, they must do so concerning your jungle." He proclaimed. Roars met the proclamation, screech chirps, and whistles from the animals of the Forrest. Never has a human come to fight in the manner of the Warden. The Jaguars roared. *"This is your Forrest Warden, your home."* Lance smiled broadly. "Thank you, my family; wish us well in our battle," Lance said in departure as the winds became more forceful. The animals backed away as he was enveloped by the winds and whisked away.

Termination

Elli spoke to Lance while he traveled in the cocoon of air. *"Hurry, brother."* She projected, sounding anxious. "What's wrong?" Lance queried. *"The Mother."* was her short reply. Feeling the speed increase, Lance landed back home on Chief Mountain. He cast about for his sister. The trees spoke to him. *"The mistress of the earth awaits you at the Sacred Falls of the running eagle."* The trees exclaimed in a deep, sonorous, ageless bass voice. Lance headed for the waterfall that is sacred to the Blackfeet Nation.

Small animals paused as he walked through the woods. The birds raised their voices in praise. *"The warrior, the Warden, the defender."* They sang in praise as Lance made his way to his sister. Ellie sat with her back to the falls. The air was crisp, and the sky was cloudless. Lance got the impression that the weather directly contradicted his sister's feelings. Rounding a bend, Lance came upon his sister, who, upon seeing him, jumped up and ran into his arms. "Brother, I was frightened for you during your battle," Ellie explained. Lance smiled, releasing his sister. "No need, El. The Mother supported me far beyond my expectations." Lance declared. Ellie's face turned serious. "I want you to tell me about it. However, we have another problem." Lance grew tense. "What's happening, sis?" Lance probed. Ellie took a deep breath. "I think the Mother has gone insane," Ellie shared. Lance expressed doubt. "El, She was there for me when I needed her. I don't think she is that far gone," Lance paused momentarily before asking. "What would make you say such a thing?" Ellie looked around her. This weather pattern is of my making; elsewhere, it is in a disturbing flux." She pointed out. "Meaning?" Lance pushed. "I feel a tremendous build-up of pressure as if The Mother is considering unleashing her full wrath upon humanity. Right now, she has unleashed contra-storms," Lance had a blank expression. "I mean that she is creating unnatural storms for the region. She has created Tornados in Alaska, A major earthquake in the Dakotas and midwest, and the temperature is dropping below freezing in tropic zones, China is flooding, Europe has a massive heatwave." Lance embraced his shivering sister. "Calm yourself, Nokomis; together, we shall aid The Mother," Lance said calmly. Ellie gave him a hard stare. "And how are we supposed to change the mind of an angry spirit? We can't console or embrace and tell her everything will be alright, so how should we do that?" Ellie exclaimed. "I know," Lance began softly. "That there is purpose. I know that we were given a gift to achieve that purpose. I believe in you, my sister. I believe you will uncover the path to Mother's salvation." Lance claimed as his voice rang with confidence. Ellie looked at her brother and smiled. "You are so corny." She teased. Lance smiled, happy to see his sister calm again. "I know." He knocked in return. Ellie sat again; this time, she faced the legendary falls and spoke aloud. "To the spirit of the grate Weasel, the one called Running Eagle, and I call upon you to guide me. Guide me to the place of the Mother who has shrouded herself as if in mourning. Guide me so we may help her stabilize and recall her duty to life." Ellie prayed. Moments later, she was passed before a thick fog covered them. So thick that Ellie could not see her brother. Slowly, the mist cleared, and Ellie and Lance were shocked and appalled by the sight that greeted them. At the foot of a starved, leafless, shriveled tree sat Terra. The Mother of the Earth looked haggard, exhausted, and furious.

"Mother." Ellie cried. Lance dropped to his knees, and fury rose in his stomach. Ellie touched his arm to steady him. Terra took no notice of their presence. Terra cackled as she prepared for an assault of massive destruction. Ellie saw The Mother raising the world's waters in her mind for a global Tidal wave sweeping across the Continents and destroying all life.

Ellie sat to compose herself; Lance quivered with anger. After a moment, Ellie stood and walked to a pool that was still with occasional ripples. Ellie realized the waves were sporadic, timed events. As Ellie stared, intrigued, she noticed the timing and realized it was the pulsation of a resting heartbeat. The realization shook Ellie. This was the heartbeat of the Grandmother of all! Ellie motioned for Lance to stand beside her. Lance obliged with a look of curiosity. Ellie motioned for them to kneel. To Lance's surprise, Ellie began to sing. "You who tamed the rock and brought the grass and the flocks. You who brought the air we breathe and the water that was our nursery and now sustains us. We all upon Gia, the great Mother, to hear our plea." Ellie sang. The pool began to stir, the waters of the pool gathered upon itself, and the water form of Gia stood before them. Ellie and Lance put their face to the floor in homage. The liquid voice of Gia was heard for the first time by mortals.

"Rise, my children. You have done us a service, Nokomis, and you, Nikoskoa, the Warden. Brave and bold, leading my children in battle. I charge you to go and tame the storms that rage; we shall be with you." With that charge, Lance was lifted off to tame the storms that Terra, in her pain, unleashed. Lance struggled in the air with storm fronts as he persuaded them into harmony. Seeing how Lance confronted the issue, Gia was pleased and looked upon Ellie, who was still kneeling, but this time beside Terra. "Your brother is wise." The Grand Mother of the world observed. "It was our upbringing, great one," Ellie responded. Gia's watery figure seemed to smile. *"Yes. I see the progression from your grandparents on you fought for us."* Ellie Looked up at Gia. "We forever shall, Mother," Ellie affirmed. Gia nodded.

"You know what to do then." She stated flatly. Ellie was confounded momentarily, but the notion dawned upon her like a sunrise. Kneeling beside Terra, Ellie began to sing. Her song was of seedlings budding roots and insects that dug around them so they got equal amounts of air and water. She continued her theme of life. She sang of birds and their eggs of growing grass, some that decided to bind and become trees, and how the trees gave oxygen to the land dwellers. She sang of the innocence of the newborn of all species, including humanity. She sang about how all animals in their youth were sometimes playful and, at other times, foolish. Still, the loving parent is always guided, never abandoning her children, and through correction, not elimination, we aid them in attaining the goals set before them. humanity had the hardest of goals, as the mandate claimed that society had the potential to sit amongst the Creative forces. Ellie, who had her eyes closed, slowly opened them to see Terra staring at her. Ellie quickly released the hand she had grasped while singing. The shifting colors of Terra's eyes held warmth; the homicidal stare was gone, and Terra looked up at the figure of her Mother. "Are you well, child?" Gia inquired.

"I am." Was the simple reply. "Very well then." With that simple observation, Gia receded into the waters. "Brave child. You and your brother have been of service to me and your species, as well as your planet. No one will believe what happened; they will make up some lies as is their manner. I, however, shall always remember, and if humanity takes another ten thousand years to achieve enlightenment, so be it. Because of your efforts here today, humanity will have that opportunity to achieve its ultimate goal, and in those days, I shall raise your names and deeds, and your names shall live forever. Now, I leave you to go and correct the damages I've caused." Ellie watched as Terra spoke, and the emaciated look transformed. Terra stood majestic. Vibrant green eyes, rose red lips, draped from shoulder to waist in a rainbow. Terra graced Ellie with a smile, then vanished.

Tribe

Clouds raced across the sky, partially obscuring the sun. John spotted an owl slowly walking toward the house of Terry and Diane. The tribal Chief was deeply concerned for the twins. Alsoome, the tribe medicine woman has had disturbing dreams, and the Chief was on his way to inform their parents, who had become important members in their own right by assisting in cleaning the lands and its lakes. As John approached, Terry opened the front door and greeted him. "Mino kidebawak neetopew." John smiled, listening to Terry's pronunciation. "A morning greeting to you as well, my friend." Your language skills are improving." John observed. "As are yours." Terry replied. "How may I help you, my friend?" Terry inquired. John motioned to a couple of chairs that sat on Terry's porch. Sitting, Terry offered John a beverage, which John politely refused. "Well then?" Terry urged. John took a moment. "I do not know what to make of this information, but I thought it was something your wife should know." John said softly. Diane stepped out of the house with cups of coffee as if on cue. Handing them to the Chief and Terry, she sat and stared at John. "What wisdom has the spotted owl for us?" She inquired. John ginned. "You are kind, but it is less wisdom and more confusion and concern." John began. "The Alsoome has not been able to contact Nokomis, so she reached out to Nikoskoa." John explained using the tribal names of the twins. John looked at Diane with concern. Terry touched John's arm lightly. "Tell us, my friend." John took a deep breath. "The Alsoome says she feels the heat of battle. The Warden has awakened and calls upon his powers to open conflict with powerful entities. I cannot see the battle's outcome but feel the Warden's rage. I ask you to join us in the lodge with the rest of the Elders to try contacting any chosen to see if we can aid them in any way." John reported. Diane nodded. "Of course, we'll be there. Ellie has gone up Chief Mountain." She disclosed. John frowned. "It is a hard climb." John pointed out. "We can go to the lodge and chant and hope for communication or go up the Mountain and find Ellie ourselves." Diane exclaimed. "It would seem as if My wife has her heart set on seeing her daughter." Terry chimed in. John nodded. "So it would seem. If that is how you wish to handle this, I suggest we take the day to pack whatever we may need." John recommended. "Pack?" Diane asked. "We don't know the location of Nokomis. It may take a few days." John clarified. Terry rose from his chair. "We will do as you advise, Chief." The old Chief nodded and walked down the pathway. Diane looked at her husband. "Terry." She began. Terry hugged his wife to comfort her. "Don't worry, sweetheart, we will find her." He tried to reassure her. "It's not finding her that I'm concerned about." Diane exclaimed. Terry nodded in understanding. "We've raised special children, my love; Lance and Ellie have grown powerful. I know this is not something we expected; who would? Who Could?! I know they have become a force to reckon with between the two." Terry pronounced proudly. Suddenly, they froze. "Did you hear that?" Terry asked. Diane shook her head. "Hear what?" She probed. "Shh." Terry insisted. After a moment of silence, even Diane heard the sound. "Is that bleating?" Terry asked. Diane ran to the door, filled with apprehension. She flung open the door. "Lip Dancer!" She shouted. The mountain goat stood outside her door. Hearing his wife, Terry rushed out the back door into their small garden and yanked on some high-fiber plants. Walking back into the house and to the front, Diane filled a bowl of water for Lip Dancer. Terry put the plants before the Goat, who bleated his appreciation. Drinking and feeding refreshed the mountain goat. "Well, my friend, how is our daughter?" Diane asked the Goat. Lip dancer dug his head into Diane's lap, bleating softly. The gesture reassured her that Ellie was safe. Terry entered the house and brought out some partially packed bags. Lip Dancer stood up, gently bit on Diane's sleeve, and tugged on her. "What is it, my friend?" Diane asked. The Goat bleated and tugged. "She wants you to mount her." The voice of Chief John explained. Turning, Terry exclaimed. "I didn't even hear you!" John smiled. "It would seem as if Nokomis sent him for you." He explained, indicating Lip Dancer. "You do not need the packs." John advised. "But," Diane challenged. "No buts." John insisted. "Dress warmly; I suspect the friend of Nokomis will take you straight to her." Diane looked at her husband. "She did come down from the mountain on her." John pointed out. Diane nodded. "Very well." She agreed. With that prompting, Lip Dancer began his slow walk through the town. Watching their retreating backs, Terry commented. "It will take forever at the pace that Goat is walking; Diane will be frozen by the the time she arrives." John shook his head. "You must understand, brother, your children are part of something we will never fully understand or appreciate." John pointed out. It did little to ease the anxiety Terry felt. As Lip Dancer ambled through the town, the children rushed out to meet him. A cheerful departure met his silent entry into the village as they regarded the Goat as a blessing. Enjoying the attention, Diane thought the Goat walked more erect, practically prancing. "Lip Dancer, do you like the praise? Are you aware of the love and admiration the people have for you? She asked in awe. In response, the Goat bleated rhythmically. Diane was in awe. "You are an amazing animal." Leaving the town, Diane glimpsed back and saw children waving goodbye. When the last of the children faded from view, the scenery blurred, and when Diane turned around, she noticed they were at the foot of the mountain. "What in the…" Diane didn't finish her sentence as Lip Dancer revealed why she was named so. She bound up the mountain. Thin cracks of rock were her purchase. Sure-footed, she jumped from lip to lip with otherworldly agility and speed. It took longer to walk out of the village than every step afterward. Reaching a spot three-quarters up the mountain, Lip Dancer found a small path and stepped onto it. Following the path, they came to a serene beauty of pools, wild grass, and a lone tree. Beside a pool, Ellie sat in meditation.

CHAPTER 16

The Greeting

Diane dismounted the Goat, who immediately ran to some sweet grass that grew beside a pond. Watching the Goat eat, Diane marveled over her appetite. When she employs her travel powers, it consumes much energy." Ellie explained. Diane whipped her head around at the sound of her daughter's voice. Ellie stood in front of her Mother. "Hi, Mom." It was a simple greeting. Diane swept her daughter into her arms and began to cry. Ellie held her silently. After a moment, Diane pulled back at arm's distance. "Let's get a good look at you." She clucked in a motherly fashion. "You look beautiful but tired, sweetheart," Diane observed. Ellie smiled gently, understanding the parental observation. "What?" Diane teased. "No complaints about me hovering over you?" Diane challenged. "No, Mother. In conversing with Nature, I now understand the meaning and intensity behind a mother's love, and I would beg your forgiveness for all that I've put you through. Diane cried as she embraced her daughter. "You and your brother have been a blessing to your father and me, speaking of which, many rumors are speaking of war and…" Ellie held up her hand in a gesture of silencing. Diane fell quiet, awestruck by her daughter's authority. "Mother, the rumors are true. Nature is ill and has taken our assault on her very personally." Diane nodded in understanding. She and her husband have been trying to warn people for most of their professional lives. It was not until the outright rejection of their findings that brought them to the Blackfoot tribe in search of a relatively safe place to raise their children, and now she looked upon the fruition of that decision. "My brother went to the Amazon forest, where he engaged in battle with the devastators," Ellie reported. A look of worry was clear on Diane's face. Ellie reached out and touched Diane's hand in a gesture of reassurance. "Do not worry, Mother." Ellie coaxed. Diane's look hardened. "How can you say you understand a mother's love yet ask me not to be concerned about my son putting himself in harm's way?" Diane demanded, thinking, *"My daughter has become too detached; she does not care if her brother lives or dies!" Diane sadly considered.* Mother, do you think Lance was in danger? Nothing could be further from the truth. Lance has THE MOTHER on his side. All of Nature obeys the command of their general; Lance has the power of Nature's Warden. Ellie proclaimed with a sense of majesty. Diane glanced at her daughter. "Power?" She probed. Ellie nodded. "Whatever he needs, I, through Nature, have provided. Diane squinted at Ellie. "How did this come about? How did you receive this power?" She asked dubiously. "As you know," Ellie began. "Lance and I loved to go exploring on Chief Mountain; during one of those explorations, I was meditating by a stream when I heard moaning. I followed it and found a being that looked very sick, but she shone like a full moon. This was Terra, Nature herself, and I saw how humanity's disregard for her health and well-being had affected her mind. She considered humans a threat to her and her children's existence, so she admonished her wayward children and began striking back." Diane looked horrified. "But if she considers us her enemy, how do you or Lance justifiably call upon her for aid unless," Diane paused, terrified. "Have you, too, abandoned us?" She queried. Ellie smiled at the misunderstanding. "No, Mother, of course not." Diane glared at Ellie. "Then how?" She began. "Do we utilize her gifts?" Ellie finished her sentence. Diane nodded. "I convinced her. I told her of our lineage, my gift of sensitivity, and our desire to aid us all. When I transported Lance to the jungles, it was by Her grace that I could perform such a task. She then witnessed your son dare to stand against powers beyond his meager strength witnessed our struggle and has taken us as her messengers." Ellie concluded. Diane sat in awe as tears streamed down her face. "Mother, why are you crying?" Ellie asked, confused by her Mother's reaction. Diane reached out, touching Ellie's hand. "It's a combination of things, baby. It's jealousy, envy, pride, and hope. I hope this all works out, but we don't want to lose you and your brother." She sniffed. Ellie smiled. "Mother, Lance, and I are nearly invulnerable, and no harm will come to us." Ellie tried to pacify her Mothers' fears. "What I'm afraid of, sweetheart, you just showed me a glimpse of, so heed my warning. Be mindful of power. You are human, and power is insidious in how it affects us. The power of Nature is god-like. Be sure to abide by Nature's law of equilibrium, and you might escape the temptations and seductive desire to use power unnecessarily."

Ellie paused at her Mother's distress. "Mother, you think I'm capable of apathy?" She asked. "I know that unless we have balance, all we have is extremism, which the exercise or expression of power loves as it becomes an excuse to utilize it," Diane demanded. Her Mother's observations took Ellie aback. "It is unsettling that you think so little of me, Mother." Diane nodded. "Of course, it is, baby, but I must give you a clear warning so you may be guarded against the siren calls of power. I don't know if THE MOTHER is helping you with this issue; perhaps you should speak with her about it?" Diane suggested. "I think you're right, Mom; the next time I converse with her, I will," Ellie mumbled aloud. "Before you leave, tell me, are you okay? Will you be okay? Is there anything your Father and I can do to help you in your cause?" Ellie smiled. "There is. First, put together a comprehensive paper on the ecological damage done since the beginning of the Industrial Age. Second, tell them the storms and natural disasters will increase with a frequency that will leave the planet uninhabitable unless the following conditions are not met." Ellie began. "You realize how we react as a species when we are threatened?" Diane inquired. Ellie cocked her head as if to say, "Really?"

Diane smirked, "Okay, just asking. "If my conditions are not met, I shall appear in all the harbors in the world and invite tsunamis to wash over the lands, and those landlocked shall know earthquakes as never witnessed before leveling whole cities. Tell them this is not a threat but a promise. If you don't start treating the world that supports you better, it will release you from the burden of life she gracefully gifted you. Go and tell them SO SAY" S THE MOTHER OF ALL!" Ellie uttered before vanishing. Diane sat there a moment, ingesting the information Ellie had shared. A moment later, Diane turned as Lip Dancer head-butted her and bleated, which Diane rightfully took as a signal that it was time to leave. She stood and looked at the spot her daughter had inhabited a moment earlier. She mused about the destiny that unraveled for her and her husband because neither she nor Terry would have ever guessed that they would raise the saviors of both Nature and Humanity. The smile of pride was wiped off as the lip dancer head-butted her once again. *"I wish we could speak as you and my daughter did."* Diane wished aloud; to her astonishment, she heard in her mind. *"As you wish."* came the mental reply. A wish Diane would later regret, not knowing how much lip dancer loved to chat. *"I am so honored that the Mother of the Nokomis would consider speaking to one as lowly as myself. You must tell me everything there is to know about the Nokomis and the Warden! Were they good children? Did they always love Nature?"*

Diane slowly walked to her home with the Goat beating at her. "I guess we should be mindful of what we wish for," Diane muttered as she approached her house. Terry watched them come. He laughed, surmising what had occurred as the Goat kept bleating at his wife, and she seemed to be listening. "Do we have a new guest?" He inquired. The lip dancer bleated loudly as it rushed into the house. The couple laughed as they entered the home. A calm breeze and a beautiful sunset painted the serene sky, and Terry smiled, knowing his children would keep watch over things.

FIN

WRITTEN BY
J.E. SERRANO

www.ingramcontent.com/pod-product-compliance
Lightning Source LLC
Chambersburg PA
CBHW040835010826
48978CB00012BB/760